VISITORS

JOHN PENNINGTON

"No Tale Tells All" originally published in the Static Movement anthology, *Speculative Long Fiction,* copyright 2011.

"Manufactured Tragedies" originally published in the Pill Hill Press anthology, *Twisted Legends*, copyright 2009.

" '69 Shadow" originally published in the Pill Hill Press anthology, *Daily Flash 2011,* copyright 2011.

"Food of the Gods" originally published in the Pill Hill Press anthology, *Dark Things V,* copyright 2010.

"Topper McCliffton..." originally published in the Pill Hill Press anthology, *Daily Bites of Flesh 2011,* copyright 2011.

"None More Black" originally published in the Pill Hill Press anthology, *Haunted,* copyright 2010.

"Room Service" originally published in the Pill Hill Press anthology, *Love Kills,* copyright 2010.

"Daggoth the Destroyer" originally published in the NorGus Press anthology, *Strange Tales of Horror,* copyright 2011.

"Long Time Listener" originally published in the Pill Hill Press anthology, *Big Book of New, Short Horror,* copyright 2011.

"Behold, a Pale Horse" originally published in the Pill Hill Press anthology, *Daily Flash 2011,* copyright 2011.

"29 Down" originally published in the Rainstorm Press anthology, *Whacked! An anthology of Murder,* copyright 2012.

Copyright © 2009, 2010, 2011, 2012, and 2013 by Jonathan Clark.

For my love, Crystal, and my mother, Kim.

Contents

No Tale Tells All	1
Manufactured Tragedies	32
'69 Shadow	37
Food of the Gods	40
Topper McCliffton's Five Step Plan to Becoming a Zombie-Killin' Machine	47
None More Black: The Fall of Astral Cross	54
Room Service	67
The Shadows of All Forms that Think and Live	78
Daggoth the Destroyer	93
I Think Her Name Was...	115
Long Time Listener	120
Jimmy's Story: A Deranged Parable	128
Spies Like Us: The Wild and Crazy Rock 'n Roll Tale of Wingnut's Ride through Sex, Drugs, and Assassinations	134
Behold, A Pale Horse	152
29 Down	155

No Tale Tells All

(This is probably my favorite story I've written so far. I wrote it for inclusion in an anthology dealing with clichéd stories. I got the title from some other writer, but for the life of me I can't think of who it was.)

"wo hundred and fifty bucks!? You gotta be kidding me?"

Donald Murdoch stared at the elderly Asian man on the other side of the store counter. Upon entering the store, *Chang's Emporium of Mystical Wonders*, Donald was only semi-certain the old man was a shyster. Now, listening to his overpriced assessment of the Underwood #5 typewriter, Donald was positive of it.

"The most I'm willing to give is a hundred."

"Two-fifty is the price. Take it, or leave it," countered Chang, who, despite his ethnicity, spoke with an unmistakable New York accent.

"Okay, first, that thing isn't worth a hundred bucks for the condition it's in, let alone two-fifty," came Donald's reply, which he knew to be a slight understatement. It was closer to one hundred and seventy-five. "I'm willing to go one-fifty on it, and that's being pretty charitable."

Donald could see his attempt at negotiation was working. The old man thought a few seconds before replying. "Two hundred."

Donald's response was quick. "One seventy-five."

"One-ninety. And that's as low as I'm willing to go."

The old codger was a shrewd son of a bitch; Donald had to give him that.

"One-ninety and you throw in one of those shrunken heads," Donald said, pointing at the ghastly things that rested on a nearby shelf. He knew from the old man's silence that he was going to take the offer.

"Okay," the old man replied, seconds later.

Donald counted out the money, took his merchandise, and exited the store, glad to get out of the musty, incense filled dump. *I'll probably have to burn my fucking clothes*, he thought, as he sniffed his jacket.

The smell had indeed seeped in.

He'd only gone there on advice from his shrink, who seemed to think that trying new things and visiting new places would help to break him out of his crippling writers block. Including the old man's shop, Donald had visited two flea markets, a tattoo and piercing parlor, three art galleries, a dance studio, and a class on 1940's Big Band music. Helpful if he ever wanted to tap dance like Danny Kaye or get his scrotum pierced by a bald chick with tattoos on her head.

Not so much for helping him write his next book.

He actually would've left the old man's dingy dive straight away had he not seen the typewriter sitting out in plain view. There wasn't anything too special about the typewriter itself—Donald had two of the same model already and they were in much better shape. There was just something about this one, and he knew once he saw it that he had to have it. And it had nothing to do with the old man's crazy story behind the thing.

When Chang told him, Donald thought the story sounded like the plot of one of those god-awful horror novels that were all the rage. *Whatever you write becomes reality.* Those were the man's exact words when describing it to Donald. He believed the old man's story about as much as he believed in Superman.

Twenty minutes after exiting the store, Donald pulled his car into the driveway of his stylish, upper-middle class home, the fruits of having two *New York Times* bestsellers, back to back. He wasn't exactly rich, but he had more than enough to keep himself going for quite a while. At least until he finished his new book, which he hoped would put him into a new tax bracket. All he had to do was write it. But with a deadline looming in a mere eight months and no solid idea of what it was he was going to write about, Donald was in a bit of a hard spot.

He made his way inside the house and into his den, set his new prize on one of the end tables, and almost immediately forgot about it. Sitting down at his desk, he readied himself to do some writing.

After staring blankly at his computer monitor for close to an hour, he rose from his chair and left the room, closing the door on his way out.

A week and a half went by before Donald even made a passing glance at the old typewriter again, which still sat in the exact spot he'd left it. He picked it up from the table and gave it a good, thorough look. Upon his second inspection, Donald discovered the machine was in much better shape than he originally thought. In fact, this one looked to be in better shape than either of his other two.

Donald wiped it down with a rag, removing all the dust and grime that had collected on it after years of neglect and inactivity. He set it down on his desk and slid a sheet of paper through the carriage. Time for the real test.

The quick brown fox jumps over the lazy dog. Donald typed out the sentence, taken aback by the typewriter's smooth responsiveness. The thing was a hundred years old, but it typed like it was new out of the box. *Maybe it did have supernatural powers*, Donald amusingly thought to himself.

He scrolled a couple lines down the page and began to type again. *Donald Murdoch had a lovely vase of daisies that sat upon his dining room table.* Immediately after typing the sentence, Donald felt a flush of foolishness sweep over him. He had no vase of daisies in his dining room. He had no flowers in the house at all.

Before he could admonish himself any further for even slightly believing the old Asian shopkeeper's story, his phone rang. Upon answering it, he instantly whished he hadn't. It was his literary agent. And there was only one thing he could want. An update on the new novel. The new novel which Donald barely had outlined.

"No, no. It's going great. I should be about halfway through it by the end of the week," he lied into the phone. During the rest of the ten minute conversation, Donald told no less than a half-dozen more lies, before cutting the call short, claiming he had to get back to work.

He hung up the phone and stared at his blank computer screen for several minutes, then switched his gaze back to the old typewriter. *Too bad this damn thing doesn't have the power to write this book for me* was one of his last thoughts before he closed his eyes and succumbed to his mounting exhaustion.

Two hours later, Donald awoke from his nap with a nasty kink in his neck and a raging headache. He walked to the kitchen and grabbed a bottle of aspirin from the cupboard, followed by a bottle of beer from the refrigerator, figuring if he wasn't getting any writing done, he may as well get drunk. He popped a couple of aspirin from the bottle and chewed them up, washing them down with a healthy gulp of beer. He rifled through the small stack of mail sitting on the kitchen counter.

Bill. Junk mail. Junk mail. Bill. Ju-

Something in his peripheral vision caught his eye. Donald turned to look in the dining room.

There, in the middle of his dining room table sat a lovely vase of perfect daisies. Donald neither felt, nor heard, the beer bottle slip from his grasp and clang off the hardwood floor. He stumbled, astounded into the dining room, desperately trying to comprehend what it was he was looking at. The vase was a deep blue color and had some sort of scene painted on it.

An orange fox jumping over a sleeping brown dog.

Donald reached out and touched the vase, the feel of its cool, glassy surface beneath his fingers established that he wasn't hallucinating. Everything he'd typed had become reality.

He looked around the room, as if there would be some miraculous clue that would unravel the mystery which presented itself. *There's no way this could be real*, he thought. *Could it?*

He walked through the house and checked all the doors and windows, scanning each room for anything that looked out of place. Everything was locked up tight. Nothing seemed out of the ordinary. But Donald wasn't surprised. He knew there was only one explanation that made any sense.

Back in the den, the typewriter sat on the desk, paper still in the carriage. Donald half expected it to have magically disappeared and was a little surprised when he saw it. He did notice one small difference, however. The sheet of paper was now blank.

He checked his desk and wastebasket, thinking he may have taken the sheet he'd typed on out and replaced it with a fresh one. But even as he was checking, he knew that wasn't the case. He had left the sheet of paper in the typewriter. The very same blank sheet that now stared back at him. He hunched over the machine and typed.

Donald's front door flew open.

He waited and listened. Complete silence. He walked to the front door. Nothing. Closed and locked, just as it had been moments earlier. He went to the living room and sat down on his couch. From there he had a clear view to the front door. He turned on the television and waited.

And waited.
And waited.

⊛ ⊛ ⊛

Donald opened his eyes. The room had grown darker, as dusk began to set in. He had no idea how long he'd been asleep, or how long he'd been waiting for that matter. The only thing he was sure of was that his front door was wide open.

He sprang from the couch, nearly falling as he did, and half jogged to the front door. He looked it over and saw no signs of forced entry. If someone had broken in they would've had to have done so with a key, and Donald had the only set. He stepped outside into the cool of the November air and looked around, trying to make sense of everything.

I fell asleep. Nothing happened until I fell asleep.

He felt the cold seep into his bare skin and he turned to head back inside.

The door was closed behind him.

Donald was positive he didn't shut it on his way outside and he was fairly certain he didn't hear it latch.

Must've been the wind, he thought, as he opened the door and went back inside. The last thing he had on his mind was how his front door got closed.

Thoughts raced through his head as he made his way to the den. He could have virtually anything he wanted. Anything that his vivid mind could dream up.

Gotta be careful about this, Donald thought. *Can't go too overboard right off the bat. I've got to start small. Don't get too carried away. This could get out of hand if I'm not careful. One second I'm basking in money and sex, the next minute the world is being overrun by fucking zombies or some stupid shit like that. That would be bad.*

Very bad.

Sitting down behind his desk, Donald already knew one thing he wanted. He began to type. *Donald Murdoch's new novel, My Perfection of Humility, is an international bestseller. It has been printed in five different languages and has brought the author an enormous amount of wealth and fame.*

He sat back in his chair and read over the paragraph, a slight feeling of trepidation coming over him, which quickly passed. *That was, by far, the easiest book I've ever had to write,* he thought, chuckling to himself at the notion. He stared off into space for several moments and thought of anything else he might need or want. There was only one thing he could think of.

Someone to share his new fortune with.

Donald's girlfriend, Simone Hanson, is a beautiful woman in her mid-twenties. She is of Swedish and Brazilian descent. His fingers flew across the keys, as he'd obviously given a lot of thought about his ideal dream girl. *She is five foot eight, one hundred and twenty-five pounds, with a perfect hourglass figure. Her silky blonde hair runs down past her shoulders. She is quick-witted, with a sly sense of humor. She is very smart; her IQ is in the one-thirty range. She is also a fantastic cook and a huge Boston Red Sox fan.*

And she is madly in love with Donald.

He paused and read over his new creation. He forgot one small detail.

And she loved to have sex.

It was nearly midnight when Donald finally retired to bed. To celebrate his new life he ordered pizza from his favorite place and watched a science fiction movie marathon that happened to be on television. It would be his last night as a bachelor. His last night alone. Tomorrow he'd wake up next to a beautiful woman and have all the fame and fortune he could ever imagine.

He climbed into bed and almost immediately fell asleep. His dreams that night were strange and vivid, nothing in them made any real sense. They were simply short bursts of nonlinear, surreal scenes, full of beauty and fear.

Sunlight poured through the window, blinding Donald, as he opened his eyes for the first time since the previous evening. Except for himself, the bed was empty.

He slumped down on his pillow, dejected and upset.

How could it not have worked? he thought. *I'm so fucking stupid. How did I fall for something so idiotic? I probably dreamed it all. I ca-*

Out of the blue he noticed the faint aroma of bacon and eggs. He leaned up on his elbows and listened to the footsteps creaking their way up the stairs.

She came around the corner carrying the tray that held the source of the delicious smell. She was even more beautiful than what he'd imagined she would be. She was wearing a pair of tight fitting shorts that revealed her long, tan legs, and a small tank top, which revealed even more of her than the shorts did.

Simone.

"Good morning sleepyhead," she said, in a cheerful voice that was pure bliss to Donald's ears. "I made you some breakfast. I figured you could use it after last night's 'extracurricular' activities."

"Uh...yeah. Ye-yeah," he said, trying to sound as

if he wasn't confused.

She put the tray down on the dresser and sat down next to him on the bed. "Are you okay?" she asked, gently touching his forehead. "You sound sick."

"No... no. I'm fine. I just had some... crazy dreams last night. I'm not quite awake yet." He nodded toward the tray. "All that for me?"

"Yep. It's your favorite. Bacon, over-easy eggs, wheat toast, and a tall glass of orange juice."

"You not hungry?"

"Yeah, but I had to wait for you to wake up to get what I wanted for breakfast," she said, before sliding beneath the covers to claim her meal.

Donald sat on his living room couch and thumbed through his 'new' novel. Two sex-filled days had passed and this was his first real break from Simone. The pair had barely left the bedroom in that time, although it had been almost three years since Donald had been with a woman, so it was easy to see why. After the morning's 'activities,' Simone promised to make him an extra special dinner and had gone out to pick up a few things, leaving Donald to his own devices for the afternoon.

He found the book laying on an end table in the living room. He immediately noticed the title on the front cover and decided to give it a look, figuring it might not be a bad idea to know a bit about the story, considering he's the one who *wrote it*.

Reading through the book, Donald was surprised it had become a best seller at all. It was the most bloated, self-serving, pretentious piece of crap he'd ever read. Even the author's photo on the back cover reeked of self-importance.

But it was making him a shit load of money, so why should he care?

Simone returned around four o'clock and began making dinner. She wanted to surprise Donald, so she all but barred him from coming into the kitchen. After a couple of half-hearted, playful attempts, he conceded defeat and returned to his book.

An hour passed before Simone called Donald into the dining room. A deep red cloth covered the entire table; the dishes of food were laid out in a big circle in the center. In the middle of the circle of food sat a beautiful decorative center piece, consisting of a vase full of roses and several tall candlestick holders, the burning candles in them lighting the room more than adequately.

Simone looked even more elegant than the dining room did, in her skimpy, red mini dress, which left little to the imagination. Donald wondered if he would even be able to make it through dinner.

"Wow. This looks incredible. You... look incredible. I think I might be a little underdressed, though," he said, referring to his attire—pajama pants and a Jimi Hendrix tee shirt.

"I think you look just fine. If you ask me, you're overdressed," she said, tugging on the elastic waistband of his pants.

Donald chuckled. "You know, I'm gonna need an IV drip to replace all the body fluids I've lost to you in the past couple days."

"You ain't seen anything yet baby," she replied, leading him to his seat.

"You gotta be careful with me. I'm advancing in years," he said, sitting down.

"Well, this should help keep your strength up." She pointed to each of the dishes on the table. "Baked butternut squash, creamed sweet peas, brown sugar glazed carrots, and the main course—red meat, sautéed in creamy mushroom gravy."

"Red meat? That's pretty vague. What kind?"

"Well... it's kind of a secret family recipe. If I told you, you might think it's gross and not even give it a try."

"Come on. I promise I won't do that. You can tell me."

"I'll tell you what—you try some of it and tell me how you like it. Then I'll think about telling you what it is. Deal?"

"Deal."

Simone dished out the food onto their plates and they began to eat. Everything was as delicious as Donald thought it would be, especially the meat. It was extremely tender and the mushroom gravy blended perfectly with the meat's natural flavor.

"This is really good,' Donald gushed. "You said this was a family recipe?"

"Yeah," Simone replied. "It was passed down from my great-grandmother. It's changed a little over the years. The mushroom gravy is something I added, but there're several things you can do with the meat if you cook it right. The problem is the meat's kind of... hard to come by. It's pretty rare."

"What is it?"

"Are you sure you want to know? You might not like it after I tell you."

"I'm sure. Besides, I already said I liked it."

"Okay." Simone paused, still not sure if she should tell him. "It's... from the calf. The smaller part of the leg. It's much more tender."

"You mean *from a calf*? Why would you think I wouldn't like that?" Donald asked, a hint of surprise in his voice.

"I don't know... I just... Didn't think you'd be so... accepting. You're not mad, are you?"

"No," Donald chuckled. "Why would I be mad? It's just veal. Hell, I thought you were gonna tell me it was monkey brains, or donkey penis, or something like that."

Simone looked at him quizzically. "What are you talking about?"

"What do you mean?" he returned, not exactly sure what she was asking.

"What's *veal*?"

"Well, that's what it's called. Veal. You know, young cows? That's wh—"

"Wait, wait," Simone interrupted. "I don't think you understood. It's not cow meat."

Donald looked confused. "But that's what a calf is. It's an animal."

"That's not the kind of calf I was referring to. I said *the calf*. Not *a calf*."

It didn't take Donald long to comprehend what Simone was telling him. "Wh—Are you telling me this is... this is... a..."

She didn't have to answer; the look on her face told Donald all he needed to know.

"Oh, God. Oh... oh, God! Ohhhh fuck! I think I... I'm gonna be sick."

"I knew I shouldn't have told you," Simone sighed, getting up from her chair and moving to Donald's side. She stroked his back and head with her hand, and tried to calm him down. "It's okay," she said in a soothing voice. "It's alright. Just breathe."

Donald did as she suggested and breathed deeply, in and out. But the smell of the food, that only moments ago made salivate with hunger, now turned his stomach with nausea.

"You're a... a... you're a fucking cannibal?"

Simone stopped touching him. "Is that a problem?"

By the tone of her voice and look in her eye,

~ 13 ~

coupled with the fact that there was really only one way she could've come across fresh, human flesh, Donald figured it would be a good idea to choose his next words carefully. He switched gears and put on an acting display Brando himself would've been proud of.

"Well, I mean... no. No. It's just... you know... It's a little unexpected, that's all. You know I would... I'd do anything for you. Just... give me a heads up next time."

"Good," she said, her tone returning to normal. "I knew you'd be understanding about this. My last boyfriend just couldn't come to grips with it. It didn't work out too well between us."

Donald wanted to ask about the boyfriend, but quickly decided that now just wasn't the time. "Well... My therapist is always telling me to try new things." At that moment, Donald decided to fire his therapist.

Simone pulled his chair back from the table and straddled him. "For some reason all this talk about food is making me really horny," she said, rubbing her hands up and down his chest. "What do you say we skip the main course and go straight to dessert?"

"What, uh... What's for dessert?"

She leaned in close to whisper in his ear. "My mouth, wrapped around your big... fat... c—"

"Oh, hey," Donald interrupted, gently pushing her back. Just the thought of having a known cannibal's mouth around certain parts of his male anatomy didn't sit well with him. "I'm, uh... not feeling that great tonight. I think I'm gonna... pass on the sex."

Her tone sharpened. "It *was* the food, wasn't it?"

"No. No, I was already—"

"Don't lie to me," she said, now full on menacing.

"I swear. I was trying to put on a good front because I knew how hard you worked on the meal," he lied, praying he was convincing enough. "And I think I might be... slightly allergic to carrots. They've never set well with me."

His ruse worked. She softened and began to stroke his hair again. "Why didn't you tell me? I would've understood."

"I didn't want to disappoint you. You were so excited about making me this special meal... I just didn't want to let you down."

"Ohhh, you are so sweet," Simone gushed, her eyes welling up slightly. She threw her arms around Donald and hugged him hard. "I love you."

"I love you too," he replied, still fighting back the urge to vomit.

After Simone had gone to bed for the evening, Donald spent most of the remaining night puking up the human flesh he'd consumed. It wasn't nearly as easy as he thought it would be though. He tried forcing his finger down his throat, which just made him gag and his eyes water. To finally achieve the desired effect, he had to go to the source of his discomfort. Just the sight of the Tupperware container in the refrigerator brought his stomach contents up into his throat. Pulling the lid off of it sealed the deal.

Once he'd purged his guts of the unholy food, Donald retreated to his den. He sat down behind the old black typewriter and thought about how he should handle the situation. All he knew for sure was that Simone had to be out of his life. No matter what he wrote, or how he changed her, he'd never be able to trust her again.

His initial thought was to have her run off with

some other guy. Some other guy who just happened to live in a far-away country. But the thought of her knowing who he was, and considering what he knew about her, he quickly ruled out that prospect. And there was the pretty good chance that she'd eat more people. Donald didn't need that kind of stress weighing on his conscience.

He deliberated with himself for nearly an hour before it became abundantly clear what needed to be done. Being that she was a cannibal, and quite possibly a psychopath as well, he didn't see them having much of a future together. And as long as Simone was out there in the world, he would never feel totally safe.

She had to go.
Permanently.

Donald awoke the next morning and made passionate love to Simone. She may have been a cannibal, but she was still his dream girl, and she was incredibly hot. And, as this would be the last time he was ever going to see her, he figured why not go out with a bang.

Simone showered and left not long after, just as Donald had written the night before. Soon a police officer would notify him that Simone had died in a one-car collision. After that, he would create a new Simone.

One that didn't enjoy eating people.

A couple hours passed as Donald waited to be notified of Simone's passing. He cleared his refrigerator from top to bottom, scrubbing it down with bleach and throwing out all the food inside it. He was just finishing up the last scrub down when he heard the knock on his front door.

Two plain clothes police officers stood on his front porch. Although their badges were clearly visible clipped onto their belts, Donald would've been able to pick them out on their clothes alone. They both wore the archetypal cop suit—plain, color free, and looking like they had just come off the rack at the local Goodwill. *Christ*, Donald thought, *I thought that was just some cliché. Where the hell did these guys shop at, Cops-R-Us?*

Donald opened the door. "Yes?" he asked, pretending as if he didn't know why they were there.

"Mr. Murdoch?" asked the senior officer, who Donald thought resembled an older, more rugged version of Steve McQueen.

"Yes, I'm Donald Murdoch."

"Mr. Murdoch, I'm Detective Wayne and this is my partner, Detective Grayson," the older detective said, motioning to his younger, African-American partner. "Do you mind if we come inside and have a word with you?"

"No, no. Not at all," Donald said, sounding as unassuming as he could.

He led the two cops into the living room and offered them something to drink. The older detective, Wayne, replied that a glass of water would be great. Donald was in the kitchen getting it when the younger detective spoke up for the first time. "Hey, wait a second. You're that writer, aren't you?"

Some detective. "Yeah, that's me," Donald called from the other room.

"My wife loves your books," Grayson continued. "I'm more of a... Tom Clancy, John Grisham kinda guy myself. Never been a fan of the artsy stuff. No offense."

Donald walked back into the room and handed the glass to Detective Wayne. "None taken. It isn't everyone's cup of tea. So, what can I help you with?"

Detective Wayne pulled something from his inside jacket pocket. "Do you know this woman?" he asked, showing Donald Simone's driver's license.

"Yes. She's my girlfriend. Why? What's wrong?"

"You may want to sit down Mr. Murdoch," Wayne said.

Donald did as the detective suggested. "What's wrong?" he asked, feigning surprise.

"I'm afraid we have some bad news," Grayson chimed in. "Your girlfriend, Miss Hanson, she was involved in a car accident. She did not survive."

"That can't be. I just... I just talked to her a couple hours ago. This can't..."

"We're very sorry for your loss," said Detective Wayne.

"We do have some questions for you though, about your relationship to Miss Hanson," Detective Grayson added.

"She was... just my girlfriend. We hadn't known each other all that long. There's not much to tell really."

"Well, we still have to ask."

"Okay. I'll answer whatever I can."

"Actually, I think it would be best if we did this down at the station," said Detective Wayne.

"Why? I'm not under arrest am I?" asked Donald, now genuinely concerned.

"No, no. Nothing like that," Wayne answered. "We... just need to clear a few things up."

"Am I going to need a lawyer?"

"That depends," Grayson answered. Donald could tell he was the bad cop of the two.

"On what?"

"On whether or not you're hiding something from us," Grayson answered again.

"Look Mr. Murdoch, if you've got anything to tell

us, now would be a good time," interjected Detective Wayne.

"No. Nothing. I don't even know what this is all about," Donald said, perplexed by what was going on. As he followed the two detectives out the door, apprehension overtook him and he knew whatever was going on, it almost certainly wasn't good.

The interrogation room was exactly like the ones seen on television, right down to the mirrored window. No one told him anything upon his arrival at the station; they just took him to this room and sat him down behind the big, metal table. He sat in the room for close to an hour before the same two detectives who picked him up came through the door. Detective Wayne was carrying a square shaped package, which he tossed onto the table, before sitting down across the table from Donald. Grayson, the bad cop, remained standing.

"You know what that is?" asked Detective Wayne, no longer sounding like the good cop.

"No. Should I?" Donald answered.

"What that is, is twenty years in prison. That's pure, one-hundred-percent, uncut, Columbian nose candy. You know where we found it?"

Donald swallowed, pretty much knowing the answer, but not wanting to be told. "No," he replied.

"In your car. But you probably already figured that out on your own, since we got you down here and all. No, it wasn't that we found the drugs in your car that makes us suspicious. It's *where* we found them. You know where that was?"

Donald shook his head.

"On the inside of your car door. That's an old

~ 19 ~

drug trafficking trick. If it's done like that, the only way to locate the drugs is to use the canines. That is unless you have an accident. Then the drugs are real easy to find.

"Now, I'm gonna make this real clear for you Mr. Murdoch. We found four of those in your car. All together that's eighty years. And I'm sure with a good enough lawyer and good behavior, you could probably shave that down to thirty or forty. But let's be honest, you don't want to go to prison, do you Mr. Murdoch?"

"N-no. No I don't."

"Good, good. Now I'm going to ask you some questions, and unless you wanna spend the rest of your life tossing another guy's salad, you damn well better answer them truthfully. You got me?"

Donald nodded, unable to muster any words after the detective's vivid description of what would happen to him if he lied. There was no way he'd make it in prison.

"How well did you know Miss Hanson?"

"Not... not real well. We hadn't been going out for very long."

"How long exactly?" asked Grayson.

"I... I'm not sure," Donald stalled, knowing he couldn't tell them the truth. "A few weeks I guess."

Grayson pulled a photo from his jacket pocket and laid it down on the table, in front of Donald. "Have you ever seen this man?"

Donald looked at the photo. It was of an older man, who was of Spanish decent. "No, I've never seen him."

"You sure?" asked Wayne. "Take a good look at it. You sure you've never seen this man?"

"I'm not lying to you. I swear to God, I've never seen this man. What is this all about?"

"The man in the photo is Ernesto Herrera,"

replied Detective Grayson. "He's a South American drug lord. In addition to drug trafficking, he's also been tied to acts of murder, torture, rape, and cannibalism. Guess who his grand-daughter is?"

Grayson slapped another picture on the table. Even though she was younger and her hair was shorter, Donald recognized Simone right away.

Donald was about to say he was going to be sick before his body beat him to the punch. Vomit spewed all over the table, with the two detectives catching some of the spray, as it exploded off the table.

They were none too pleased about the development.

Donald lawyered up quickly after the vomiting episode. At that point it didn't matter though. His puking prowess gave the cops enough reservation about his involvement, and they decided to let him go for the moment. He wasn't completely off the hook, but he was much better off than where he started. He hurried from the police station in a mad rush, fearing they might change their minds about letting him go if he took his time.

He wasn't twenty feet out the door when he felt his cell phone vibrate in his pocket. It was his agent.

Fucking great was the only thought that popped into his head as he answered the call.

"Okay Martin, I already know what you're going to say, so just save it. I had no idea who the girl was, or that she was using my car to smuggle coke. This is all just... It's a misunderstanding, is all."

"What the fuck are you talking about?" asked Martin from the other end of the phone, clearly confused as to what Donald was saying. "Coke smuggling?"

"Yeah. I assume that's why you're calling me, right? Jesus, Marty, I'm in some serious shit here."

"Oh, you're in some serious shit alright, but it doesn't involve coke smuggling bimbos. Let me ask you something. When did you come up with the idea for 'My Perfection of Humility?' "

"Hell, I don't know. A year ago, maybe two."

"Are you absolutely sure about that? Think back."

"Christ sake, what is it with the goddamn questions today? Yes, I'm fucking sure. It wasn't more than a couple years ago. Why the hell do you need to know this?"

"I need to know it Donny, because this asshole from bum-fuck, Montana is claiming you stole his story."

"So? We've run into these kind of people before Marty. All they want is a quick payout. Why are you wasting my time with this? Just get rid of him."

Martin paused for a second. "He's got a thirteen year old copyrighted manuscript, Donald. I've checked it against your book. It's word-for-fucking word."

Donald stopped dead in his tracks. He started to say something, but found he couldn't utter a single comprehensible word. Legitimate plagiarism in the literary world was a fucking death sentence and Donald knew it. He'd *almost* rather take prison time for coke running, as opposed to being blacklisted for being a plagiarist. *Almost*.

In four days his life had turned into some crazy *Twilight Zone* episode, sans the weird music. Without saying another word, Donald hung up the phone and hailed the first taxi he saw.

He had to get back home. Back to the cursed typewriter, to see if he could salvage anything he had

~ 22 ~

left of his life.

The scene was a full on cop show when the taxi turned onto Donald's street. Donald was on the verge of panic until he realized the cop cars and ambulances weren't parked in front of his house. It was one of his neighbors, who lived a few houses down. Mr. and Mrs. Nelson, both retired and in their sixties. *One of them must've had a heart attack or something,* Donald theorized as the cab pulled up to his house.

He got out of the car and paid his fare, briefly turning to look at the scene unfolding behind him.

Detectives Wayne and Grayson were on the scene in fresh, unsoiled suits, and they were heading his way.

"Busy day," said Wayne, meeting Donald in the driveway.

"What's going on with the Nelson's?" Donald asked.

"We were hoping you could tell us," Detective Grayson piped in.

"Well, I don't know what I can tell you."

"Where were you yesterday?" asked Wayne.

Donald sighed. "I was at home. All day."

"Anyone who can vouch for that?"

"Yeah. My dead girlfriend."

The look on Wayne's face to his reply let Donald know the detective didn't appreciate his sarcasm.

"What about her?" asked Grayson. "Was she here with you all day?"

"No. She left to do some shopping that afternoon."

"And you're positive you've got no one who can

~ 23 ~

verify your whereabouts yesterday?" asked Wayne.

"You know what guys? I'm through answering questions without my lawyer present," Donald answered.

"Fair enough. I don't suppose you'd mind then if we take a look around your place?"

"Yeah, I do mind."

"That's fine. But we're just going to come back with a search warrant. And it's not going to be a problem getting one, considering you're smack dab in the middle of a cocaine smuggling investigation, and soon to be murder investigation."

"Murder?" Donald asked.

"Yeah. Mr. and Mrs. Nelson were found murdered in their house this afternoon, not long after we picked you up," Grayson butted in. "Medical examiner placed the time of death sometime yesterday. They were all cut up. Mutilated really. Several parts of their bodies were cut off. We can't seem to locate them."

The detective's words sunk in and it became clear to Donald whom he'd eaten the previous night.

"You sure you don't want to let us in the house?" Grayson asked.

"Yes, I'm sure," Donald said to the men, stone faced, before turning and walking away.

"We'll be back Mr. Murdoch. Soon. And with a warrant," said Detective Wayne. "Don't make any plans."

Unbeknownst to the two detectives, Donald had already made plans. And they didn't involve sitting around in his house, waiting to be arrested.

Fifteen minutes later, Donald was hurrying

through the woods behind his house, gym bag over one shoulder and the typewriter in both hands, certain he was a fugitive from the law. He'd disguised himself a bit before he left, donning a baseball cap and an old pair of reading glasses. It wasn't the best disguise, but Donald figured it should create enough subterfuge for him to rent a small motel room to lay low for the night. Hopefully everything would be back to normal by morning and he could get back to leading his dull, boring life.

Donald exited the woods and looked out at the two-lane highway. He was relieved to be out of the dense forest; the light was starting to fade fast, due to the gloomy, overcast sky. He began to walk southbound, away from the city. He stuck his thumb out in desperation. He'd never hitchhiked before and was amazed to discover how easy it was to land a ride, after only trying for about ten minutes. An old man in a beat-up pickup truck stopped and Donald jumped in, glad he didn't have to walk the twenty miles to the next town.

The old man made a little small talk during the half-hour trip. If he recognized Donald, he didn't let on that he did. Donald wasn't surprised though. The old man didn't look like much of a literature fan, given the Dale Earnhardt decal on his back windshield and the chewing tobacco spit cup that rested on the dashboard. He asked Donald what he was doing hitchhiking, to which Donald replied with the first thought that popped into his head—he was heading to Boston to become a poet. The old man asked if they had a school for that out there.

The beat-up truck stopped in the parking lot of the run down motel. Donald thanked the old man, got out of the cab, and made his way into the front office. Five minutes, and thirty dollars later, he checked into his room. It wasn't a complete dump, but it was without a doubt the worst place he'd ever stayed.

He set the typewriter down on the dresser and wasted no time in getting down to business.

Donald Murdoch walked past Chang's Emporium of Mystical Wonders, never stopping to buy the cursed typewriter. His life returned to normal and he was no longer wanted by the cops.

And he was no longer a plagiarist.

Donald sat down on the bed and switched on the television, flipping to the local news station to see if there was anything on about him or Simone.

Not only was there something on both of them, but it was the top story of the night.

He listened as the mildly-attractive newswoman replayed the day's events back to him—Simone's car crash, the cocaine, the gruesome discovery of the Nelson's, and the breaking story that his world-wide best-selling novel was nothing more than plagiarism. They even interviewed the man who he'd unknowingly plagiarized.

Ten minutes was all he could take. He started to flip around the channels, waiting for the drowsy feeling to hit him, glancing at the typewriter every so often.

Nearly five hours passed before he was finally embraced by the arms of sleep.

The typewriter was gone.

It wasn't on the dresser, on the floor, or on the nightstand. It was nowhere to be found in the motel room.

Sunlight beamed in through the windows, illuminating Donald's good fortune. He showered

~ 26 ~

and dressed quickly, so eager to start the new day that he never even turned on the television set or sat down to relax. He phoned a taxi from his room and headed over to the mom and pop dinner, which sat across the street from the motel, to grab a little breakfast. His taxi arrived twenty-five minutes later and he departed. He briefly considered returning home, but instead decided to go downtown. He had to see the typewriter back in the store for himself; to be sure the nightmare was truly over.

It took nearly an hour to get downtown, as traffic during that time of the morning, on a weekday to boot, was atrocious at best. Donald, not wanting to wait in the traffic, had the cab driver drop him off a few blocks from the store. After a few moments of walking, he arrived at the storefront window of *Chang's Emporium of Mystical Wonders*.

The typewriter sat exactly where it was located when Donald originally bought it. He laughed to himself and breathed a sigh of relief. The nightmare was over.

Time to get a drink.

Donald walked a couple streets over to a small bar he sometimes frequented, fully intent on getting completely wasted. It was a dark, dingy place; a place for hard drinkers to get away from the strains of life. There were only a half-dozen people there, including the bartender, when Donald came in from the beautiful, bright, sunny day.

He walked straight to the bar and sat down at one of the stools. "Hi Melissa. I'll take a pitcher and a double shot of Southern," he said to the female bartender.

"Oh... uh... Sure Donny," she replied, a look of surprise on her face. "How's it... uh... been going?"

"You wouldn't believe the past couple days I've been having," he replied, watching her make the drinks. He glanced up at the muted television mounted to the wall behind the bar. It was playing a commercial for some male enhancement drug.

Melissa set the drinks down in front of Donald and he gave her a twenty dollar bill. He slammed the shots back, one after the other.

I really needed that, he thought, moving his gaze back up to the television set. He was surprised to see his face staring back at him from the screen. A sinking feeling settled into the pit of his stomach as he read the crawl on the bottom of the screen. *Best-selling author, Donald Murdoch, suspected in drug trafficking, murder, cannibalism, and plagiarism.*

Oh, fuck.

He looked around the bar again to notice everyone staring at him. Melissa had her cell phone up to her ear.

He shot up from the bar stool like a bottle rocket, falling to the floor in the process. He hurriedly picked himself up and stumbled out the front door.

Donald ran blindly down the street, the only thought in his head was one of self-survival. He could hear the police sirens somewhere off in the distance, and he knew he had to get out of the open.

There was only place he knew to go.

The door to the old man Chang's store flew open with a flash, as Donald charged through it with a huff. Chang looked square at him, and before Donald could get a word out, he spoke up.

"I was beginning to think you were never coming back."

"What?" asked a confused Donald.

"You made it almost three weeks. That's gotta be the record," Chang said. He moved out from behind the counter, locked the front door, and flipped the store sign to *closed*. He pulled the window blinds down so no prying eyes could see inside. "It only took me five days. The guy before me only took two."

"What are you talking about? How do you..."

"I'm talking about why you're here."

"I don't know why I'm here. Everything's different. This isn't how I wrote it. It's... it's..."

"It's all fucked up is what it is. Yeah, I know. Been there, done that. What's the saying, 'nothing's ever as good as it seems?' "

"What? You mean you knew what was going to happen?"

"Well yeah. How the hell do you think I ended up here? You think I'm really Asian? Do I fucking sound Asian to you? I'm an Irish-Italian kid from the Bronx. I look like this because it's part of the deal."

Donald tried to speak, but couldn't comprehend what Chang was trying to tell him. The old man could tell he was totally confused.

"Let me ask you something," Chang continued. "Why do you think, out of all the places you could've ducked into a couple'a seconds ago, you decided to come in here?"

"I... I don't know," Donald answered.

"I can tell you why. You came here because it chose you."

" 'It chose me?' How can that be? It's... it—"

"Look, you're thinking about it like it's just a regular fucking typewriter, jack. Last time I checked, a regular typewriter can't make two bags of money appear on your doorstep. Yeah, that's what I wrote for. Problem was, the money came from a bank robbery. Needless to say, I was in the same position you're in right now, almost twenty years ago. I was given a choice—leave my life exactly the way it was or take over as the things new 'caretaker.' "

" 'Caretaker?' " a still puzzled Donald asked.

"Yeah," the old man laughed. "Don't ask. The guy I took over for told me the same thing. I'm just relaying the message. To tell you the truth, I've never found a single thing on it, and I've been looking for twenty years. Probably 'cause the only people who know about it are like me and you. The only thing about it I can tell you for sure is that it's kinda like a demented version of a genie's lamp, or a monkey paw. And you can never get away from it. And you can never leave it. At least not until you find someone willing to take it from you."

"But why? Why can't you just pack up and leave?"

"In short—you'll die."

"How could you know that?"

"Hey man, it's just what I was told. I wasn't too keen on testing the validity, if you know what I mean."

Donald walked slowly around the shop for several minutes in complete silence. "But why was everything different than what I wrote last night?" he finally asked. "Everything should've been different."

"That's an easy one," answered Chang. "The answer is the reason why you're here now. You obviously wrote that you didn't want the typewriter in your life anymore. That's the inevitable conclusion. After you write that, you can't change anything else. And besides, even if you could change it, it would turn out to be something worse than before."

Donald shook his head. "I can't believe you'd allow somebody to buy this thing knowing what you know. How the hell could... I..."

"Oh, now I'm the bad guy. Let's see you go twenty years waiting for somebody to buy this fucking thing. See how well your morals hold up then. And besides, it's not like you or I had any choice in the matter. Like I said before, it chose you. I could've charged you a thousand dollars for that thing and you would've paid it. When you first saw it you probably had a thought in the back of your mind that said 'I have to have it,' didn't you?"

Donald nodded.

"Guess what? I had the same thought go through my head too. The guy before me told me the same thing. You think that's some kinda weird coincidence?"

Donald shook his head and sighed. He slumped against the wall and slid down to the floor, surrendering himself to his current situation. "So what do I do now?"

"Now... you gotta make the choice," answered Chang. "Leave your life the way it is and suffer the consequences, or you choose to become the new caretaker and you take over for me."

"What happens to you?"

"I have no freakin' clue. First time for you, first time for me. I gotta say I'm curious to find out. If you choose to take over, you gotta type it out like regular. You go to sleep... The next day... Well, I'm sure you can guess the rest." Chang paused.

"So... are you in or out?"

The old man Chang, formerly best-selling author Donald Murdoch, sat behind the counter of his new shop, wondering how long it would be until someone relieved him of his burden.

Manufactured Tragedies

(This is the first story I ever sold. It was a great day getting the email that I was now a published writer. It was an even greater day when the finished books came in and I got to see my story in printed form.)

Richard pulled his knife from the dead girl's body and thoroughly wiped the handle. Finding his way around campus in the dark had been much more difficult than he'd expected, and it took him almost fifteen minutes to remember where he had killed her.

Her boyfriend's body was laying ten feet away, his throat slashed. It had been an easy kill for Richard—he waited in the shadows for the young man, and then snuck up behind him when he found his dead girlfriend.

The kid never had a chance.

Of course, that's the way Richard wanted it. He didn't dare risk a straight up confrontation with the younger, more physical, college male. To do that would've amounted to suicide.

No, Richard had planned his work well, and he worked his plan even better.

He pulled up the sleeve of his black sweatshirt to check his watch. 2:30 A.M. He was running way ahead of schedule, with only a couple more tasks to do before he could leave.

He made his way back to the Dean's office, located in Freemont Hall. The place was unlocked, but then again, every building Richard had been to that evening was unlocked. It was one of the reasons he chose Hoxford in the first place—easy accessibility.

Richard arrived at the Dean's office and went inside. It was a big room, with several windows, which let in just enough light for him to do his work. The place was covered in hardwood—wood floors, walls, furniture.

A large ceiling fan hung in the middle of the room, and from it, with the help of a makeshift noose fashioned from an extension cord, dangled the lifeless body of Julia Summers. When Richard first strung her up, he wasn't sure if it would hold her weight. She was already dead, of course. He couldn't take the risk of hanging her alive—that would have surely brought the fan down.

He took the bloody knife and put it in the girl's hand, making sure her prints were all over it. There had to be someone to blame. In his time working with law enforcement, he'd found that cases which looked like they were the "open and shut" type were more often than not treated as such—open and shut.

It wasn't like the shows or movies on TV. In the real world, Richard knew, there were no third act

~ 33 ~

surprises where the true killer was revealed and everything was magically sorted out.

In the real world, innocent people, more often than not, got the short end of the stick.

After making sure Julia's prints fully covered the knife, Robert took the weapon with him to the Dean's massive oak desk and carefully placed it on top. He retrieved a piece of paper from his hip pocket, unfolded it, and placed it on the desk as well.

It was Julia's final farewell. Part confession, part suicide note, detailing the crime and why she'd committed it. Richard picked up the knife in his gloved hand and slammed it into the note, affixing it to the desk so it would be easy to find.

He then went through the room, checking and double checking to make sure everything was in order. After ten minutes of meticulous work, he concluded everything was fine and left the room without looking back.

On the mile-long walk to his car, Richard neither passed, nor saw, another person. It was colder than normal for late October and he was pleased when he finally made it to his automobile, glad to be out of the cold.

He got in and began his six hour drive home.

Richard pulled his BMW into his driveway at a few minutes past ten o'clock. The morning was ending, and it looked like it was going to be a beautiful, blue-sky day. He got out of the car holding his breakfast, which he picked up along the way, and made his way into his modest, middle-class house.

Once he got settled in, Richard sat down in his favorite armchair and turned on the TV. He ate his breakfast while searching through the channels, looking for anything on the murders.

It didn't take him long to find something.

"College Campus Halloween Massacre" read the headline on the screen, as aerial images of the crime scene were shown. Richard turned up the volume, munching on his biscuits and gravy.

"The early reports we are getting from the scene suggest that one of the students or faculty members may be responsible for the murders," came the anchorwoman's voice through the television speakers. "Once again if you're just joining us, the campus of Hoxford University has been rocked this morning with the news of a multiple murder/suicide, which investigators say took place sometime late last night or early this morning. Details at this time are sketchy, but early reports suggest at least four people are dead and a student or a faculty member may be involved. We'll have more on this story as soon as more information is made available."

With that, the local news station switched over to a story about the economy, annoying Richard. A college campus murder story was much more important than anything to do with the economy.

He switched the channel over to an all-news station, in the middle of a commercial break. While he waited for the news to come back on, Richard got up from his chair and walked over to his telephone to check his voice mail. He had one message from his literary agent informing him that his new book had just cracked the top ten bestseller list.

Richard smiled at the good news, just as he heard the anchorman report the grisly news from Hoxford University. After a few moments of watching the program, he was a little dismayed they hadn't mentioned him yet.

Richard picked up the remains from his

breakfast, listening intently to the reports and various theories as to what may have happened. He was in his kitchen, tossing the last of his scrambled eggs into the trash when he first heard his name. He hurried into the living room to see his face emblazoned on the screen.

"As you may know," began the anchor, "Richard Jenkins is the famous psychic who, on the 'Quincy' show, predicted that something like this was going to happen. Once again it looks as though he was right, just as he was with the Flight 261 explosion and the Philadelphia office fires, which combined killed over two hundred people. He also recently helped police in Georgia locate a convicted rapist, who had abducted and killed several women in the area."

Richard looked at his photo on the screen, recognizing it as the same one that was on the back jacket of all of his books. The picture had looked much better to him when he'd first chosen it. Now he wasn't so sure.

As he continued to watch the news, he decided to fire his stylist.

'69 Shadow

(The protagonist of this is based on the Sunday comics character, The Phantom. I love the idea of a hero whose mantle is passed down, generation to generation, giving the appearance of a hero being immortal. A legend. It's not stated in this story anywhere, but the surname of the heroine is "Shadow.")

"Thanks for stopping," said James, as he climbed into the passenger seat of the black '69 Chevelle. "I've been waiting forever for someone to come along."

Behind the wheel sat a pretty, fair-skinned woman, her straight, dark hair flowing down past her shoulders. "Where you headed?" she asked.

"Albuquerque," he replied, closing the door.

"Well, I can take you as far as Santa Rosa. I'm Max," said the woman, offering her hand.

James returned the introduction and shook Max's hand. "Max? I've never met a woman named Max before. Short for Maxine?"

"Nope, short for Max. Trust me, it's a long story."

The muscle car roared back to life and the pair continued along in the cool desert night.

"Albuquerque, huh? That's a way's away. What're you going there for?" asked Max.

"I'm looking for my sister," James replied.

"She in Albuquerque?"

"I don't think she ever got there to be honest. I know she was headed this way though."

"Got a picture of her? I drive through here a lot, maybe I've seen her."

James fumbled in his jacket pocket and seconds later produced a photo. He handed it to Max, who gave it a good look.

"Yeah, I've seen her," Max replied casually.

"Really? Where?"

"I met her at a bar near here. Few nights ago. She was a little too drunk to drive herself home, so I gave her a lift."

"So you took her home?"

"No, I didn't," came Max's chilly reply. "Truth is James, I killed her. And I fully intend on killing you too."

James sat in silence for a moment. "You're kidding, right?" he asked finally. "This is just some sort of sick joke."

"I'm afraid not James. It was the only way I knew to coax you out of hiding."

Max turned to look at James. He smiled at her and began to laugh.

"What's so funny?" she asked.

"I think one of us has made a serious mistake. She wasn't my sister, you know? She was my keeper. She was supposed to bring you to me that night at the bar. We've been looking for you for a long time." James opened his mouth wide, revealing his massive fangs. He flashed a devilish grin at Max. "My keeper underestimated you. It's a mistake I won't be repeating."

Max slammed on the brakes and James flew forward from his seat and smashed his face into the dashboard. He fell back into his seat, dazed and bloody, as the car skidded to a halt.

"You know, you're all alike. Always telling me shit I already know," said Max, before removing a knife from her jacket and plunging it into James' chest. He flung his head back and shrieked, his face reconstructing itself into its true demonic form. Seconds later, the creature disintegrated into dust, any trace that it had ever existed, gone.

Max pulled the Chevelle back onto the road and drove toward the horizon, ready for her next hunt.

Food of the Gods

(I cranked this story out in a couple hours while watching "Sunday Night Football," beating the deadline for an anthology I wanted to submit it to. I love mysteries and most of the stories I write I try to build as mysteries, whether they're horror, suspense, thriller, etc. This one is no different.)

Charlie Hathaway led the small group of survivors through the broken wasteland that used to be downtown Indianapolis. There were five of them in all, including Charlie. It had been six years since the outbreak, which turned most of the world's population into flesh eating monsters. The initial term given to them was "the infected." Charlie preferred the more practical term—zombies.

"Hold up," he said, stopping at the corner of a

dilapidated building. He peeked around the corner to make sure it was clear. He saw nothing on the moonlight-drenched street. They quickly crossed and stopped to rest, ducking behind an old, burned-out van.

"How much further is it?" asked Mark, a young man in his twenties, who was accompanied by his girlfriend, Kari.

"Not much further," replied Charlie. "We just gotta get across that bridge." Charlie pointed at the bridge he was referring to, which set over a small river, a few hundred yards away. "Our camp is set up over at the zoo. You know where that is?"

Everyone in the group replied positively.

"Good. If anyone gets separated then you know where to go," said Charlie, as he looked around, making sure it was clear. He glanced back at the group. Ruth, an older woman in her sixties was nursing her swollen knee and breathing heavy.

"Are you good? Can you still go?" he asked.

"Yes," she said. "I should be able to make it."

"I'll keep watch on her if she falls behind," said Wesley, a young, strapping African-American man.

"Alright," said Charlie, "It looks clear, we'd better get moving."

The group moved quickly toward the bridge, navigating the clustered, car-filled street. Fifteen minutes later, they stood at the foot of the bridge. What they found when they got there was not encouraging.

It was crawling with zombies.

They ducked behind a car and Charlie gave them the plan.

"Stay low and move quick," he said. "We'll use the cars for cover. Stay behind me. If anything happens, run for it. I got something set up on the other side that'll keep them off of us. Okay, let's go."

~ 41 ~

They weaved their way through the cars, moving slowly and quietly, to avoid alerting the zombies. The horde was concentrated more in the center of the bridge; once the group made it that far in, their progress slowed to a crawl. Several times they had to wait long periods just to make it a few feet, the threat of death hanging over them with every step.

The journey across the bridge took them over a half hour, but finally they neared the end. Thirty more feet to go and they were home free, for there were no zombies in sight at the end of the bridge.

"Okay, looks like we made it. Now we've just got to—"

Charlie's words were cut short as a zombie grabbed Wesley from behind and bit down into his neck. The man screamed, alerting the horde on the bridge. They immediately took notice and headed toward the group.

"Run!" yelled Charlie.

Everyone ran frantically for the end of the bridge, the zombies not far behind. Ruth stumbled and fell, screaming as she went down. The horde pounced on her, the ones not ripping her apart continued the chase.

The remaining three made it to the end of the bridge and Charlie pulled a lighter from his pocket.

"Get back," he ordered, picking up the Molotov cocktail he had hid off the side of the road earlier in the evening. He lit it and tossed it in the direction of the oncoming horde. The bridge exploded into flame, repelling the zombies, driving them back.

"Come on, let's go," Charlie shouted to Mark and Kari, and the three of them took off in a fast sprint toward the zoo's front gates.

They entered the zoo grounds and Charlie led them to the aquatic animals building, locking the door behind them.

"Oh my God, that was too fucking close," said Mark, still out of breath from all the running. Kari was sobbing, in shock from the events at the bridge.

"Are either of you hurt?" asked Charlie.

"No... no, I'm fine," answered Mark.

"What about you?"

"Wh—what?" asked Kari, still in a daze.

"Did you get bitten?" Charlie asked, forcefully.

"Hey, come on man, lighten up. Leave her alone for a sec," said Mark, coming to his girlfriend's defense.

"I'm sorry. I don't mean to be pushy, but we can't afford to let the infection spread in here."

"N—no, I'm fine," Kari answered finally.

Charlie sighed loudly. "Good," he said, before turning on the lights. "Come on, I'll show you around."

"So, how long've you guys been here?" Mark asked, as he and Keri followed Charley down a long hallway.

"A little over a month. We move around a lot, from city to city, looking for survivors. Food," replied Charlie.

"Well, I'm glad you came along when you did. We were starting to run really low on supplies. I don't know how much longer we would've made it."

Charlie offered no reply to Mark's statement and kept walking in silence.

"How many people do you have with you?" asked Kari.

"Twenty-three, including me," replied Charlie.

"That's not very many," said Mark. "How long did you say you guys have been doing this?"

"A couple years. Our food supply ran out where we were originally from, so we had no choice but to move around. We used to be about fifty strong, but we lost some people in our travels."

~ 43 ~

Kari tugged at Mark's arm and he turned to look at her.

"I don't like this Mark," she whispered to him. "Something's not right here."

"We're fine, Kari," Mark whispered back. "Don't be paranoid. The guy came half way across the city to help us."

"Yeah, but... I don't know. Something just doesn't feel right."

"It's okay. Everything's fine. We're gonna be safe now."

The hallway opened up to a big room, which housed a large, shallow pool directly in the middle of it. There was a strange odor that permeated throughout the room. Mark and Kari both noticed it immediately. Charlie paid it no notice.

"Smells like something died in here," said Kari.

"Yeah, we had to clear the place out when we first arrived," said Charlie. "Dead animals, mostly. As well as a few... undesirables."

" 'Undesirables?' What do you mean?" asked Mark.

"It's easier if I just show you," Charlie replied. "Follow me."

He led them down another hallway, which ended at a pair of double doors. When they arrived at the doors, Charlie removed a set of keys from his pocket and started to unlock them.

"Hey man," said Mark. "I don't think we ever thanked you properly."

Charlie turned to face Mark, who had his hand extended for Charlie to shake.

"Thank you. You really saved us."

"You shouldn't thank me just yet," Charlie said, leaving Mark's hand empty. "Kari was right, you know? There is something wrong with this situation."

A sinking feeling came over Mark, as Charlie

finished unlocking the doors. "What are you talking about?" he asked.

"I told you that we search the towns we're in for survivors and food. Well, that's not entirely accurate," Charlie said. "We do search for both, but it's the distinction between the two that kind of gets lost in translation." He flung the two doors open and the couple gasped in unison at the terror that met them on the other side.

The room was dimly lit, but all of its ghastly details could be made out easily enough. In the center of the room set another large pool, not unlike the one in the first room they entered. Above the pool hung several human bodies strung up by their arms. Some were dead, some were still barely alive, all in various states of decay. Bite marks, scratches, and puncture wounds littered the bodies, which allowed their blood to seep into the pool below. The sickening stench of death that emanated from the room was instantly nauseating, much worse than the foul smell from the previous room.

Mark took Kari's hand and quickly turned, only to find the hallway blocked by several men, all staring intently at them.

"I thought you said there were four of them?" asked one of the men.

"I know I did. The goddamn zombies make it difficult to do anything anymore," Charlie answered. "These two will just have to do till I go back out tomorrow night."

"What?" asked Mark. "What the hell do you want from us?"

"What do we want?" Charlie mockingly returned the question. "I thought it was very clear. We can't feed off the dead. We require live, fresh meat."

Mark and Kari turned back toward Charlie.

"And I'm sorry to be the bearer of bad news,

but..."

Charlie paused and revealed two massive fangs protruding from behind his upper lip.

"You're the fresh meat."

Topper McCliffton's Five Step Plan to Becoming a Zombie-Killin' Machine

(I like writing goofy stuff from time to time. I love being irreverent, but most of what I write doesn't lend itself to that, so it's fun to get to write things like this when the situation arises. This is the longer, uncut version. And I swear I had not seen "Zombieland" before I wrote this.)

My name is Topper McCliffton. Some of you may have heard of me. For those of you who haven't, I'm a Libra, I hail from the great state of Texas, and I kill zombies. I kill lots of zombies. As a matter of fact, I'm the best zombie killer in the continental United States (I ain't ever been to Hawaii or Alaska). But I didn't get to this point overnight boys and girls. No, no, it took years of practice, and with my help you too can become an ass-kickin', shit-talkin', zombie-killin', machine.

Now in my travels, everybody I've come across has one thing in common: they're all just tryin' to survive in this world. I hear it everywhere I go. They're either trying to survive, or just barely survivin', or thinking about survivin'. Well, you know what I say to that?

I say fuck that. This is our goddamn planet. It's time to take back what is rightfully ours. Fuck just survivin'. I don't want to live with these meathead-motherfuckers in my backyard, tryin' to eat little Topper Jr. while he's playing on his swing set.

I mean this is gettin' outta hand people. I've been all over this great country and I've heard and seen all kinds'a crazy shit. People keeping these meatheads as pets, tryin' to teach 'em stuff, treating 'em as if they were real people. I even heard about people fucking 'em. Jesus H. Christ people! They're fuckin' zombies. They're dead. As in not living anymore. I'll tell ya, we need to get our shit together people and mobilize, or we're gonna "survive" ourselves right outta fuckin' existence.

And that's why I've come up with this five step plan, which if followed, will give you all the tools you'll need to kick some serious zombie ass. So, what do you say we get started?

STEP 1: DON'T BE SENTIMENTAL. JUST KILL.

Question: You come back to your safe house to find your mother turned into a shit suckin' zombie. She comes at ya about to chow down on your throat. What do you do?

Answer: You cut her fuckin' head off. Simple as that.

It sounds cold, I know. But let's face it, it's not

like it's gonna be some kinda family reunion. She's not coming over to give you a big hug. You have to learn to detach yourself emotionally. I don't care who it is—wife, husband, mother, father, girlfriend—IT DOESN'T MATTER. You might have the best girlfriend in the world—good cook, nice body, good dancer, cups the balls—all that shit. Once she turns, none of that matters. The only meat from you she's gonna be interested in gobblin' down is your fuckin' liver. And I don't know about you, but my liver is just fine right where it's at.

So once again, don't be sentimental. Bash their heads in, break their necks, shoot 'em in the face. Whatever your preferred method of killing them is. You gotta look at it like this—you're doing them a favor.

Now killing zombies ain't the hardest thing in the world to do. You give any old retard a gun and he can kill some zombies. It's what you do when you *don't* have a gun, that's what separates the men from the boys. When you're forced to go native on their asses. And that's what we're gonna go over in step two of the plan.

STEP 2: NO GUNS, NO PROBLEM!

I've killed hundreds, if not thousands of zombies, and I'd say that less than half were killed by guns. Why's that? It's real simple—guns ain't scarce, but bullets are. It's like having Desi, but no Lucy. It just doesn't work. So let's not focus on guns. Besides, guns are for pussies.

Instead we're gonna focus on some very common weapons that are guaranteed, one hundred percent, zombie killin' certified. Anything that fires arrows is a good start. Bows, crossbows—whatever you can get your hands on. It's the same principle as a gun, but the ammo is reusable.

Anything that you can find that's made outta metal is good. Crowbars, tire tools, lead pipes, swords, big knives, etc. STAY AWAY FROM WOOD! Pool cues, baseball bats, sharp sticks—whatever. Stay away from 'em. This includes wood handled tools: axes, sledge hammers, hatchets, rakes, etc. Why? 'Cause the damn things are gonna break on you at the worst possible time and then you're gonna be fucked, that's why. So remember: we're killin' zombies here, not vampires (that's a whole other five-step plan). LEAVE WOODEN WEAPONS OUT!

Another type of weapon to leave out is the kind that runs on any power source other than you. I'm talkin' chainsaws, power drills, weed whackers— anything that runs on electricity or gas. And I know we've all seen the movies where the guy's running through the horde, slicin' and dicin' 'em up with a chainsaw. That's a cute idea and all. The reality's far different. In reality, the guy's chainsaw craps out on him in the middle of the horde and the next thing you know, fifty zombies are turning his ass into a cold-cut tray.

Using these things as weapons is useless. They will break on you and you *will get eaten*. Get rid of 'em.

Well, that about does it for this step of the plan. Just remember: wood bad, metal good, and never substitute machine power for back power.

STEP 3: THE ART OF RE-KILLING THE UNDEAD.

In my travels, the one question I get asked more than any other is "How do you kill zombies?" I used to think it was a dumb question till I heard it about a thousand times. The answer is you have to halt whatever little brain activity it has left in its rottin' head. In short, if you don't have a gun, bash its brains in with a blunt metal object, or cut the fucker's head off. It's pretty simple.

Of course there are variations, so get creative. Blow 'em up, spray 'em with acid, crush 'em with a car, drop a piano on 'em—however it has to be done, that's how you should do it. Just as long as it terminates those brain functions. I remember one time I used a pair of panty hose, a waffle iron, and a bottle of lighter fluid to kill one of them fuckers. And I already know what you're thinkin', "But you told us to stay away from those kinds'a weapons." That's only under perfect circumstances. When you have the option beforehand of grabbing a crowbar verses a baseball bat, go for the crowbar.

Unfortunately, it doesn't always work like that. There may come a time when you have to kill a zombie with a hair dryer. Or a spatula. Or with your bare fuckin' hands! The point is, whatever you gotta do, and whatever you gotta use to send those meatheads to zombie fuckin' heaven, that's the way it needs to be done.

Now the first three steps dealt with how you kill 'em. The next two deal with how you keep from gettingg killed by 'em.

STEP 4: DON'T BE A DUMBFUCK. KNOW YOUR SURROUNDINGS.

I don't know how many fuckin' times I've seen people get their shit ripped to pieces because they didn't know their surroundings. This is a simple, basic hunting technique that I've seen countless "zombie hunters" screw up. If you were hunting lions, you wouldn't go charging blindly into their den, would ya? No. So why the fuck would you go guns blazin' into a dark, old building without knowing what was on the inside? It's like ringing the goddamn dinner bell for Christ sake. You may as well just run in there screaming, "I taste good! Eat me!" at the top of your lungs. They're gonna pounce on you like frat boys on drunk chicks.

I want you to read the next couple sentences, repeat them to yourself about fifty times, and then you'll know half of what killing zombies is all about. Are you ready?

NEVER FACE A PREDATOR IN HIS OWN AREA, ON HIS OWN TERMS. ALWAYS—ALWAYS—LURE THEM OUT INTO THE OPEN, OR INTO AN AREA WHERE YOU HAVE THE STRATEGICAL ADVANTAGE!

If you remember those sentences and follow them, you'll live a lot longer and you'll kill a shitload'a zombies. Don't follow 'em and go in all guns blazin' like you're fucking Rambo or somethin', or they'll carve your ass up like Thanksgiving turkey.

And that brings us to the final step of the plan.

STEP 5: DON'T BE A HERO. SOMETIMES IT'S BEST TO RUN AWAY.

Zombies very rarely travel alone. Most of the time you'll find them in small packs of about twenty to thirty. Now for an experienced zombie killer like myself, twenty or thirty of those fuckin' meat sticks is pretty easy work. But from time to time, even I run into a horde I can't handle. We're talkin' in the hundreds here. At this point, no matter the situation or what's going on, your only option is to run. It's like The Gambler himself, Kenny Rodgers, said, "Know when to hold 'em, know when to fold 'em." If your wife of thirty years wanders off and runs into a big horde like this... Well, she shouldn't have fuckin' wandered off in the first place. She's zombie food. There's nothin' you can do for her, besides shootin' her to end her misery. If you try to play the hero here, trust me, it's gonna turn out bad, 'cause your chances of fightin' off a big zombie horde is about zippityfuckin'-zero. Remember—heroes don't last long in this world.

In short, run away, live to fight another day.

Well, that's it. That's all you need to know to transform yourself from just a "survivor," into a mean, zombie-killin' machine. Just remember—the country needs people like us. The world needs people like us. People who aren't afraid to grab the bull by the horns and fuck it right in the face!

Now, let's get out there and kill some fuckin' zombies!

None More Black: The Fall of Astral Cross

(Taken from the pages of

Metal Sledge Magazine)

(I love music journalism. I wish I could write it as well as some of the guys I admire. This is a faux article, written for an equally-as-faux magazine, Metal Sledge, about an equally-equally-as-faux Black Metal band from Denmark called Astral Cross. I nicked the title of the story from Nigel Tufnel of Spinal Tap fame, who was commenting on the cover of the band's "Smell the Glove" album—"It's like, how much more black could this be? And the answer is none. None more black.")

On February 26th 2010, former black metal musician Rasmus Torgrimson was found dead in his prison cell at the Hillesland Penitentiary in Hillesland, Finland, victim of a massive brain hemorrhage. Nearly half of his fifty-one years had been spent in incarceration (he had, in fact, just

~ 54 ~

finished the first of his five consecutive twenty-five year sentences). His death brought to a close a mystery which began many years ago, for everyone who had first-hand knowledge of the shocking events that occurred in the fall of 1985 is now dead and gone. A version of his band, Astral Cross, still exists today, although it's a mere skeleton of its former self. They are the black metal equivalent of Lynyrd Skynyrd, with only one original member remaining (original drummer Soren Hjelmstad, who was fired in 1984 and reformed the group in the mid-nineties).

So what happened in the remote lands of Finland, where three fifths of the band (along with a record producer and two engineers) were found brutally slain? Was it a simple case of murder, or were there more sinister elements involved? The only way to uncover the answers is to go back to the beginning.

Kvalheim Castle sits atop a high, steep hillside, looking down on the small town it received its name from. It juts from the ground like a ghostly apparition, its grey, stone walls blending seamlessly into the foggy, overcast horizon. It resembles every old, worn, clichéd castle that's ever appeared in any old horror film, down to its cracked walls and its large siege towers.

The town of Kvalheim was founded in the late 1600's, and even today remnants of some of its original buildings still stand, giving the place an ethereal, old world look that wouldn't feel out of place in a Lovecraftian horror story.

"It's very unique in the fact that the town was founded long after the castle had been built," says town historian Valdemar Eskelson. But exactly how long ago that was, according to Eskelson, is still up for debate. "We've had a few scientists come to run tests and they've determined the castle to be between four to eight hundred years older than the town, but we've also been told by the same scientists that it could be, in fact, much older than that."

Gaining access to the castle isn't as hard as say getting into the White House or Ft. Knox, but it isn't all that far from it either. After an hour of deliberation I'm allowed a brief thirty minute tour with a small group of escorts. It was the first time any outsider had set foot in the castle since the Astral Cross tragedy. The first thing I noticed upon entering the castle is how cold it was inside. The temperature difference between inside and out had to be close to ten degrees. I'm told by my escorts that it's been that way ever since anyone could remember.

My tour only included the first floor of the keep. When I inquired about why the other areas where off limits I was answered with a polite, but firm, "the other areas are unsafe." Resisting the urge to press the issue any further, I began to examine the keep. The first floor is dominated by a huge open room, with the largest fireplace I've ever seen embedded into the southwestern wall. Upon further investigation I find this room served as the main area of recording for the band. Barely visible on the dark stone walls are mysterious, rune-like carvings. At first, I thought they were isolated to the one area of the room, but as I looked around I noticed they were, in fact, everywhere. One of my escorts informed me that they are not runes at all, at least not like any known rune alphabets that have been found elsewhere. They are also the only ones ever to be found in Finland. To this day no one knows what they mean or why they are carved into the castle walls.

Several smaller rooms break off from the larger one, including one that houses the keeps main staircase. I immediately noticed the stairs not only go up, but also down. I am told by one of my escorts that this area was quite likely a dungeon of some sort and that three of the six victims' bodies were found down there.

This area, I'm told, is without question "off limits."

As my tour wound down, I asked one of my escorts, an older gentleman, why the town didn't use the castle to their advantage, as a tourism device. I gave him examples of places back in the states that have used situations like this to their advantage, such as the Lizzie Borden house in Fall River, Massachusetts or Waverly Hills Sanatorium in Louisville, Kentucky.

His response was brief and with a sincerity that chilled me to the bone. "Because this place, sir, *is* actually haunted."

The band Astral Cross has never been a stranger to controversy. Since its formation in 1981, the band has seen more than its fair share. Whether it was tales of animal sacrifice or onstage demonic rituals, controversy followed the band wherever it went. So it came as no shock to the band's former manager, Gerik Nyland, when the members came to him with their plan for the next record.

"They wanted to record the darkest, heaviest, most evil record ever made," says Nyland, who, at age 56, has been out of the music business for close to a decade. "And the only way they felt they could accomplish that was to record it in a place that was just as dark and evil."

Several locations were scouted and pursued, including Bran Castle (better known as "Dracula's Castle") and Dragsholm Castle, but due to the band's growing notoriety, they were turned down by everyone they contacted. "No one wanted to be associated with them," says Nyland. "And really, looking back at it now, I can't say I blame them." And then by mere chance (or fate, depending on what you believe) the band's bassist, Olaf Rosenkranz, was returning home from a visit to one of his relatives in Finland when he happened on the town of Kvalheim.

"He told me that it was like the car was driving itself," says Nyland. "He said there was no conscious decision on his part to go that way [toward the town]. He saw the town sign on the side of the road, just as he did every other time he went that way, but this time instead of going straight on, he turned off. It just happened." Rosenkranz took a tour of the castle that same day (as back then it was open to the public) and immediately following asked members of the town's counsel if his band could use it to record their new album.

"I heard the reason why they said yes was that they were approached by [Led] Zeppelin's management back in the '70s about using the place, and they turned them down," laughs Nyland. "They had another opportunity to catch lightning in a bottle and they didn't want to pass it up. They thought that [Astral Cross] were just another rock and roll band. They didn't know anything about [the band], which is probably why they said yes. And obviously we wanted to keep it that way."

The band assembled at Kvalheim castle on the last day of September of 1985. The band members (Torgrimson, Rosenkranz, Algot Gustason, Haldis Carsten, and Yorick Westberg) were joined by their manager (Nyland), record producer Davin Kolbeck, and two engineers, Torsten Haugstad and Ivar Bielke. The original plan was to record the album during the summer, but the band ultimately decided against it. "They wanted to do the album in October because of the significance of the month, especially in reference to Samhain and Halloween," explains Nyland. "Now as a manager, this presented a whole new set of problems for me, as doing anything during the fall in Finland was not an easy proposition, let alone working with a bunch of temperamental recording equipment. But, in the end, we made it all work."

Principle recording of the album began on October 1st, the day after their arrival. According to Nyland, no one experienced any kind of paranormal phenomenon that first night in the castle. "If anyone did, they didn't say anything to me. I, myself, slept like a rock."

Everything changed, however, when the band began their initial recording session. "They started it off the same way they started the recording sessions for the other records—with a black magic ritual," says Nyland. "They were all into some sort of devil worship, black magic type of things. They *were* a black metal band, after all. They kicked the rest of us out of the castle for what must've been close to an hour. There's really no telling what all went on in there."

From that night, Nyland says he never again felt comfortable in the castle. "It was a strange feeling, and I could sense it the first time I entered the place after the band finished their little ritual. The place was different than before. I can't really describe it, except to say that it was just an overall sense of dread."

According to Nyland, paranormal events began happening that very same night. "Little things at first; strange noises, gusts of wind, something moving out of the corner of your eye—things that could be dismissed. However, after a week or so, things started to happen that couldn't be dismissed. Objects would move around on their own. We could hear whispering voices coming from all over the castle. Several of us saw glimpses of apparitions. The situation was slowly escalating and I was beginning to feel a little uneasy about the whole situation. A few of us were actually, including a couple members of the band."

Nyland's breaking point came two and a half weeks in. During the night of October 18th, two days before he was to leave for Norway to deliver a rough mix of the album to the band's record company, Nyland awoke in his bed, unable to move. "I could feel hands all over my body, holding me to the bed, but there was no one there. I struggled to move my arms and legs, but I could barely get them off of the mattress. I could hear the whispers in my room. I couldn't make out what they were saying; it was a language I had never heard before. I started screaming as loud as I could and within a few seconds a couple members of the band busted into my room, and then it was over.

"I left that very night. I gathered all my things and I never went back."

That night turned out to be the last time Nyland ever saw any of his friends alive again.

~ 60 ~

According to police reports and statements made by both Rosenkranz and Torgrimson, on the night of October 30th 1985, the two men beat guitarist and band mate Haldis Carsten to death. The beating was beyond brutal; Carsten had been bludgeoned so badly that his spine was severed and his skull had been completely crushed.

A few hours later, the pair killed their other two band mates as they slept in their beds. Drummer Algot Gustason was brutally stabbed and disemboweled. Due to the severity of his injuries it was impossible for authorities to determine precisely how many times he had been stabbed.

Singer Yorick Westberg was found in his room face down on the floor, his throat slashed from ear to ear. The wound was so deep, in fact, that the only thing keeping his head attached to the rest of his body was his spinal column (like Carsten, he'd also been severely beaten). His genitals were also been removed, postmortem.

Throughout the rest of that day (October 31st), Rosenkranz and Torgrimson lured the other three men (Kolbeck, Haugstad and Bielke) down to the "dungeon" area of the castle and, one by one, killed them.

On November 6th, a full week after the first of the murders took place, Finnish police were contacted by Nyland after Torgimson failed to show up for a meeting with the manager. "We were actually supposed to meet on the 5th," says Nyland. "I didn't really think anything of it at the time; rock and rollers were always late, that's just the way it was. The next day when he didn't show up, or even call, I started to get a little worried. Of course, I couldn't get a hold of him, but what really shook me was when I couldn't get hold of anyone. That's when I knew for sure something was wrong and I called the police."

On November 10th, against the urging of their respective legal councils, both Rosenkranz and Torgrimson issued guilty pleas on all five counts of murder they were charged with and received the maximum sentence for each, twenty-five years.
Neither man offered any initial explanation or motivation for the murders.

Seven years following his conviction, Torgrimson hanged himself in his jail cell. His suicide note consisted of one line: "God help me."

On May 26th, 2008, nearly two years before his death, Rosenkranz was interviewed by a local newspaper about the killings. When asked about why he did it, Rosenkranz was reluctant to answer, telling the reporter, "I would like to tell you why, but I can't. I just can't." When the reporter asked him why he couldn't, Rosenkranz offered his now infamous, cryptic answer.

"Because they're still watching."

There are two schools of thought regarding the grizzly events at Kvalheim castle. The first is the completely scientific approach that Rosenkranz and Torgrimson were nothing more than the murderers they were convicted of being.

"We have murders here in the states that are far more heinous than the ones committed at Kvalheim, and none of those have anything to do with the supernatural," says world-renowned criminal psychologist David Poling. "Obviously when you're dealing with a case such as this, you are going to have certain people who want to look deeper into it and theorize, and sensationalize it for whatever their personal reasons are.

"Ultimately, however, the facts are you have two men who were emotionally unstable to begin with, holed up in a dark, isolated castle, playing extremely-aggressive music for close to a month. Now, you throw drugs into the mix (police found cocaine and several forms of psychedelics inside the castle) and you've got a pretty volatile situation brewing."

However, not everyone shares Poling's views. "Something in the castle took them over and continued to haunt them until their eventual deaths," says paranormal investigator and former priest Johan Spelman, who subscribes to the other school of thought about the case: that the two men were the victims of an ancient entity that they themselves unleashed during their time at the castle. "Given what we know about the events that took place, the idea that drugs were to blame, or that these men's childhoods or whatever else was to blame, is complete rubbish. I had the chance to talk, one on one, with Rasmus Torgrimson before he died and he was not a man who was insane or disturbed. The truth is there are certain places in this world that act as gateways to other places we were never meant to go. That is what I believe the castle in Kvalheim is and when they got there they awakened something there that was best left undisturbed."

Both Poling and Spelman offer compelling arguments to their respective opinions. Were the two men simply cold-blooded killers finally driven to their breaking points? Or were they victims, preyed upon by other-worldly, evil forces? Either could be defended convincingly and neither could be wholeheartedly discarded.

Years ago, when I was just getting started in journalism, my first editor I ever had gave me the best piece of advice I've ever gotten. He said: "Disregarding all consequences, to find the answers to certain questions, sometimes it is necessary to go straight into the belly of the beast."

I am writing this account as I sit in my apartment on the upper west side of Manhattan. It's nighttime and I have every light in my place on. I can hear cars and people outside, reassuring me that the city is alive.

That I am not alone.

It's been a week since I got back home from my trip to Finland; a week since I entered Kvalheim castle for the second time. I've only just now regained enough nerve to write about what it is I experienced. The notes I hastily took immediately following the excursion are jagged and shaky, almost completely indecipherable.

Before my second trip into the castle, I must admit, I was siding more with David Poling's theory that Rosenkranz and Torgrimson were simply cold-blooded killers—nothing more, nothing less.

Afterwards, I am convinced that Spelman may have been on to something.

It was just after midnight when I snuck back into the castle. It was my last night in Finland, so I wasn't too worried about getting caught (I figured the worst they would do was ask me to leave). Reentering the castle the second time felt vastly different than before. At first I assumed it was probably the fact that it was night and my nerves were just jittery, but little by little, a strange feeling of trepidation started to creep into every crevice of my body and I briefly thought about leaving.

But I knew that was not an option.

Using my cell phone as a light source, I located the stairs. The one place that completely captured my interest was the "dungeon," the one place that was without question "off limits."

The spiral staircase ended at a vast, pitch-black room; so large, in fact, that my cell phone light was of little use cutting through the darkness.

The first thing I noticed was the smell, that pungent, revolting, universal smell of death. It was stifling, as if someone had just recently died there. I made my way through the room, checking every corner and every wall, the white-fluorescent light of my cell phone guiding me along a few feet at a time.

I was somewhere in the middle of the room when I heard a noise behind me, the sound of a foot dragging along the dirt floor. I spun around to find no one. I thought about calling out into the darkness to see if anyone would answer, but I decided the whole thing was silly and I should press on.

I was about to turn when I saw the shadow pass through the light of my phone. A cold shiver ran up my spine like a lightning bolt, making me feel lightheaded. Nausea hit my stomach and I felt the dinner I had earlier that night start to come up. A cold sweat came over me as another shadow passed through the light of my phone, immediately followed by another.

Then I started to hear the whispers, soft at first and growing louder with each passing second. Several voices were speaking all at once, in a language that was indiscernible and indescribable. I couldn't understand what they were saying, but I could pick up exactly what their voices were trying to convey.

Anguish.

I hurried for the stairs as fast as I could. Going up them seemed to take forever, like trying to get away from the boogieman in a nightmare, only to find that you're running through quicksand. The whispers followed me all the way to the front door and ceased once I exited. I did not stop, however. I ran all the way into town and immediately checked out of my hotel. I packed my things in less than two minutes and was in my rental car and heading out of town in three.

    I drove all night to the airport with the windows up, the radio blasting and the dome light on.

    I haven't felt at ease since.

Room Service

(This was never really intended to be a short story. I wrote it originally as a play, inspired by another play called "Death Trap," which was made into the superb film starring Michael Cain and Christopher Reeve.)

The rumbling of the distant thunderstorm filled the swanky hotel room, as Sylvia laid on the king sized bed and talked to her lover on the telephone. Her perfectly-tanned, hourglass figure was barely hidden by her skimpy choice of undergarments—a small pair of black panties and a light-blue bath robe. Her long, dark-brown hair fell in silky strands past her shoulders and down her back, while her green eyes glowed with the color of an Irish hillside. To say she was beautiful was a gross understatement.

"Don't worry baby," she spoke into the phone, with a smooth, soothing voice, "Henry is as good as dead. I took care of it... I don't want to say too much over the phone, but I found somebody that will do it... Yes, he is."

Lightning illuminated the room, soon followed by the thunder crack.

"If you've got enough money, things like that aren't hard to find... Let's not talk about Henry anymore baby. I can't wait for you to get here. What did you get me for Valentine's Day?... Oh, yeah?... No, I'm not letting you do that!" Sylvia laughed. "But... if you're good, maybe I'll let you do something else... I bet you could."

The room got darker as the storm continued moving closer. Lightning flashed again.

The boom of thunder a few seconds later almost eclipsed the sound of knocking at Sylvia's door.

"Hold on baby," she said, before turning her attention to the door. "Who is it?"

"Room service," came the muffled, male voice from the other side.

"I didn't order anything," said Sylvia, annoyance in her voice.

"I know, ma'am. A message arrived for you at the front desk," the man said. "The manager asked me to hand deliver it to you."

"Are you sure you've got the right room?"

"It says here on the envelope room 205."

Sylvia let out an agitated sigh. "Alright, give me a second!" she yelled at the door and then returned to the phone. "I'm sorry baby, I gotta go. There's some asshole at the door... No, it's okay. I'll see you when you get here... I love you too. Bye."

Sylvia hung up the phone and got up from the cozy bed. She was tying up her robe when the man knocked again.

"Okay, I'm coming. Give me a fucking minute." She turned the doorknob and opened the door, ready to unload her frustration on the man.

"Now what's the big fu—"

Her words clung in her throat when she saw the face on the other side of the door belonged not to some lowly hotel worker, but instead to her husband, Henry.

A wave of panic hit Sylvia, as she tried to slam the door, but Henry was too fast for her. Using his arm, he caught the door and pushed it back, striking her in the chest and face, knocking her to the floor. He calmly stepped inside and closed the door.

"Surprised to see me?" Henry asked, looking down at Sylvia. Her robe was thrown open and a small trickle of blood seeped from her nose. "I'll take your silence as a yes."

In a swift, violent motion, Henry snatched Sylvia from the floor and slammed her up against the wall. She tried to scream, but the force of the impact knocked the wind from her and all she could muster was a whimper. Before she could regain her bearings, Henry grabbed her by the throat and covered her mouth with his other hand.

His eyes moved from her face down the length of her body. Her robe had come undone during the struggle, revealing her half-naked figure. Henry removed his hand from her throat and placed it on her abdomen. She stiffened and shuddered from his touch, as he slowly moved his hand up to one of her exposed breasts.

"You're looking very nice, babe. Keeping fit for him I see," Henry said, removing his hand from her breast and once again grabbing her by the throat. "And don't flatter yourself, either. I ain't here to rape you. To be honest, the fucking sight of you makes me sick. Oh, and I know about you guys' little plan. Yeah, I just want you to know you're n—"

Pain shot through his hand, as Sylvia bit down hard into it, turning his words into a scream.

"Help! Help me!" she screamed when he pulled his injured hand away.

"Fucking bitch!" he snarled between clenched teeth, looking down at his bleeding hand. Using all his force, he punched Sylvia square in the face. Her knees buckled at the violent impact, but before she could fall Henry spun her around and threw her on the bed, where she landed face down.

Henry walked to the bed and ripped the sheet off. He began to coil it tight, like a rope, as Sylvia struggled to remain conscious, the left side of her face already swollen and starting to bruise. With the sheet stretched taut between his outstretched hands, Henry climbed onto the bed and straddled Sylvia's back.

"I got news for you, honey. Your lover-boy has fucked you for the last time," Henry crackled, each word filled with malice.

"No... no, please," Sylvia struggled out, before Henry wrapped the sheet around her neck and began to strangle her. She grabbed at the sheet to no avail, as he jerked back, bending her backwards. She tried to scream, but could only muster a few short gasps. Henry strained against her, tightening the sheet. He could feel her body crack and pop, as he forced her back even farther, until her torso sat straight up and down off the bed.

Lightning. Thunder. The windows rattled at the boom.

Henry let go of the sheet and Sylvia's limp body fell face-down on the bed. He reached down and touched her neck.

No pulse.

He climbed off of her, sat down on the edge of the bed and thought about his next move, while inspecting his wounded hand.

Steven walked the hotel hallway, carrying flowers and a big heart-shaped candy box under his arm, and looked for the correct room door. He'd been there earlier that morning, but he couldn't quite remember his way around. It had been a couple hours since he'd talked to Sylvia and he was anxious to find her room. After a few minutes wandering the seemingly endless corridors, he found the one he was seeking. Room 205. Taped on the outside of the door was a big, red Valentine's Day heart. Steven opened the note and read it.

Steven,
Come on in, I'm waiting for you.
xoxo

He used the key Sylvia had given him and opened the door, already mentally undressing himself. The room was dark, save for the lights from the windows and the occasional flash of lightning. Sylvia was lying on the bed, completely naked, back towards the door.

"Room service," he said. "Oh ho—ho, you are a naughty little girl. Couldn't wait for me, huh?"

Steven walked over to the bed, eyes never straying from Sylvia's naked frame.

"Hey baby, I'm here. I got you something," he whispered, taking a seat on the edge of the bed.

"Baby, are you awake?"
No response.
"Sylvia?"

Steven took hold of Sylvia's shoulder and turned her towards him. Even the darkness of the room could not conceal the fact from him that she was dead.

"What the fuck?!" cried Steven, quickly hopping from the bed as if it were on fire. Sylvia's swollen, bruised face looked back at him, with white, lifeless eyes. Nausea hit him and he felt the bile in his throat. He started to turn away from the horrific scene, when lightning flashed again and he saw a shadow on the wall that wasn't his own.

Steven barely had enough time to duck the baseball bat that was hurtling towards his head at a bone-crunching rate. It smashed into the wall, getting hopelessly stuck in the drywall and wood. Before the shadowy figure could pry it loose, Steven tackled him, both men collapsing to the floor.

A brutal, savage fight ensued. Steven had been in some minor scraps before, but none of them even remotely compared to this one. This was an all-out fight to the death.

They slammed each other into the walls and furniture, the sound of thunder barely covering the ruckus they were making. The fight eventually spilled into the bathroom, with each man trading several blows, until Steven landed a punch that connected squarely with his attacker's jaw and dropped the man to the floor.

It didn't, however, stop the man from dragging Steven to the floor with him.

Once on the floor, the man tried his best to gain the upper hand, but he was too groggy and overmatched.

Seizing the man by the back of the head, Steven

rammed his face into the porcelain toilet. The man let out a muffled cry, but still did not fully surrender. He grabbed wildly at Steven, clawing and tearing at his face and anything else he could get hold of. There was no quit in him and Steven knew what he had to do to end the fight.

It was the only option.

Using all the strength he could muster, Steven shoved the man's head into the toilet bowl. The man's limbs flailed about helplessly, as he tried to free himself. Steven drove his knee into the man's back, holding him down, pushing his head deeper into the bowl.

Soon, the sloshing of the water slowed and the man's limbs went limp.

Steven held him down for a couple of minutes, until he was sure the man was actually dead. Once he was certain, he collapsed to the bathroom floor, battered and exhausted.

After taking a few moments to regain his composure, Steven picked himself up off the floor and switched on the bathroom light. He stepped to the toilet and lifted the dead man's head from the bowl.

Henry Young, Sylvia's husband.

Sylvia. He turned his attention back to the bedroom.

A knock sounded at the door.

"Room service," came the male voice from the other side of the door.

"Yeah? What do you need?" asked Steven, in as calm a voice as he could collect.

"We've had a report of a disturbance coming from this room. We need to talk to you sir."

"Uhh... we're fine. We just... we... we broke a lamp."

"I'm sorry sir, but you're going to have to open

the door and talk to us."

"No, it's... We're fine. Everything's good."

"Sir, if you do not open the door, we will open it ourselves."

Steven sighed, defeated. "O-okay. Just... just uhh... just give me a second."

Steven looked in the mirror. His jacket was ripped and his shirt was missing two buttons. His face was a maze of blood and scratches. He *looked* like a guy who'd just been in a life or death fight.

He wouldn't be able to lie his way out of this. He splashed some water on his face and hair, dried himself off, and walked to the door. He took a few seconds to calm himself, and then he opened it.

Steven was sure he was dead when he saw the gun pointed in his face. It was enormous. Solid black, with a big, black silencer attached to the barrel. The dark-haired man's wardrobe was about as monochromatic as his choice of firearms. Black leather jacket and gloves, white dress shirt, and black pants with matching shoes.

Steven didn't recognize his face, and he was sure he'd never seen him before. He wasn't ugly, but he wasn't handsome either. Like his wardrobe and firearm, he was very plain. Steven assumed this must be the hit man Sylvia had hired.

"Go sit over on the bed," ordered the hit man. Steven complied and took a seat on the edge of the bed, next to Sylvia's body. The hit man followed him, never taking his gun off Steven. He looked in the bathroom to see Henry's dead body, head still in the toilet. "Well, since I know you're not Henry, I'm going to assume that's him there, right?" he asked. Steven didn't speak, only nodded.

"I've never seen that before," said the hit man, referring to Henry. "I've heard of it. Once knew a guy who said he did it, but I ain't ever seen it. How long did it take?"

"W-what?" replied Steven, barely able to get the words out.

"How long did it take him to expire?"

"I... I don't know. A... a few seconds."

"Damn. Pretty effective. He put up much of a fight?"

Steven didn't answer.

"Yeah, hard one to answer, I know. Guess he didn't though, considering he ain't the one sitting here now, right? You ain't a pro, are you?" he asked, a sly grin breaking across his face.

"No," Steven replied.

"Yeah, I know. I'm just fucking with you," said the hit man. He walked to the chair next to the bed and sat down. "I'm gonna take a wild guess and say the dead chick next to you is Sylvia, right?"

"Yeah."

"Yeah. You didn't kill her too, did you?"

Steven let out a small sigh. "No."

"I'm just messing with you again. Doesn't take Sherlock Holmes to figure out what happened in here. Man, she sure does have a great ass though. All due respect to the dead, of course. You don't mind if I swing around there and get a peek at the front, do you?"

Steven didn't answer, although it wasn't as if the hit man was looking for his approval. He got up from his chair, leaving his pistol resting on the arm. He glanced at Steven as he walked around to the other side of the bed, looking for any sign that the scared man was going to make a play for the gun.

He never did.

"Man, she's got a smoking-hot body, doesn't she?" the hit man asked. "Her face probably looked pretty good too, before her husband beat the shit out of her, that is."

The hit man returned to his seat and sat down, placing his hand on top of his gun. "You can't really blame him though, can you?" he asked. "I mean, if I caught my wife screwing some other guy, I'd do the same. Wouldn't you?"

"Y-yeah, I guess so," replied Steven.

"Are you saying that 'cause you mean it, or are you saying it because you're afraid of what I may or may not do to you?" the hit man replied, in a cold, calculating voice. He gave Steven a look that demanded a real answer.

"I... I don't know," came Steven's reply.

"You don't know?! What the fuck kind'a answer is that?!" snapped the hit man. Steven watched him grip the pistol tighter as he spoke. "How can you not know? Look at her. If you caught her cheating on you, would you, or would you not want to kill her and the douchbag she was fucking?"

"Y-yeah," Steven replied, reluctantly.

"Fucking-a-right you would," the hit man said, relaxing his grip slightly on the gun. "It's the principle of it all. Really, if you let her get away with that... Hell, you'll pretty much let her get away with anything, right?"

Steven nodded.

"You know, it's a damn shame. Broad was good looking. You were the guy screwing her, right?"

Steven nodded again, trying to hide his growing fear.

"How was she?" asked the hit man.

"What?" Steven replied.

"In bed. Was she good in bed?" The hit man's smile returned. "I bet she was. A body like that... I bet she was a real firecracker."

"Yeah..." said Steven, as he looked over at Sylvia's nude figure.

"I thought so," said the hit man. He stood up,

grabbing the pistol as he did. He looked at the gun and checked it. Everything seemed to be in working order. He looked down at Steven. "Damn shame."

Lightning. Thunder.

Steven closed his eyes, said a quick prayer, and waited for the shot that would end his life. He felt his bladder empty, as a wave of emotion passed through his body.

Several seconds passed. There was no shot.

Steven opened his eyes.

"Doesn't look like I'm gonna get the rest of my payment, does it?" asked the smiling hit man, his pistol back in its side holster.

Relief swept over Steven, as the hit man turned and headed towards the door.

Lightning flashed.

"Oh yeah, I almost forgot."

The hit man turned.

"I didn't get your name," he said.

"I-It's Steve. Steven."

"Steve. Well Steve, I'm sorry about your girl." The hit man turned and left the room.

Steven let out a long sigh, tears streaking down his face. He looked at his urine-soaked pants and chuckled to himself. He was openly sobbing, thankful to be alive.

Suddenly, a knock came from the door and he felt every muscle in his body tense up. A male voice came from the other side.

"Room service."

The Shadows of all Forms that Think and Live

(The title of this comes from a line in Percy Shelley's "Prometheus Unbound," a line which is quite central to the plot of this story. I mainly wrote this as an experiment to see if I could write an entire story with no dialogue.)

Bradley Stratten woke in his single bed, in his one-bedroom apartment, to the annoying sound of his alarm clock, alerting him that it was time to get up and ready himself for another dull day at his boring, dead-end job. All he had to show for his thirty-seven years was a broken down knee and back, his piece-of-shit car, and a small mountain of debt. To say his life was a shambles would be understating the obvious.

As was the case on most other days, Bradley masturbated in the shower. He was finding it hard to get an erection nowadays; impotency ran high on both sides of his family tree. It wasn't as if he was in dire need to get it up however, as it had been nearly three years since he'd been with a woman and his current romantic outlook was practically nil.

He finished showering and continued on with his morning ritual. After brushing his teeth, he looked long into the mirror. His youthful good looks had faded long ago and his once vibrant green eyes were now bloodshot, weary-shells of their former selves. Set into his weathered, furrowed brow, their iris' stared back at him, dull and lifeless.

Thirty-seven years? What the fuck happened?

With that thought firmly tucked away in his mind, Bradley finished getting ready for work and left his apartment ten minutes later, heading out into the hot, Phoenix morning.

5,594 miles away in Madrid, Spain, Stefan Herrera was just finishing up his workday, with his usual hour-long train ride back to the town of Murcia. Unlike Bradley, Stefan loved his job. He was a student at the University of Murcia and worked three days a week as an intern, under the guidance of his computer science professor. He was born into a wealthy family, but unlike most of the kids that grew up in his neighborhood, Stefan's parents made sure he had to work for everything he got, instilling in him a good work ethic and moral code. It was one of the reasons Stefan didn't hang out with most of the kids from the old neighborhood.

The train came to a stop at the Murcia station and Stefan departed. Murcia was a beautiful city, with its old-style architecture and lush greenery that Spain was known for. The city was one of the reasons Stefan decided to enroll at the university, instead of going to college in his native Madrid. He exited the station and caught the tram back to the university grounds. One last stop to his dorm for a quick shower and a change of clothes, before hitting the clubs with some friends, who, like Stefan, had no classes the following day.

He met his friends around six at a small bar not far from the dorms. They liked to start the night at smaller, less crowded places. The alcohol buzz helped them integrate easier into the more populated, louder discotheques. Around ten o'clock they ended up at La Terrazza, one of the more popular clubs of college crowd. Stefan met a girl there, Megan, and they hit it off almost immediately. Based on the vibes she was giving off, he was hopeful, if not a little certain, they would be having sex later. She sported an American accent; Stefan figured her for a tourist, although it was possible she was an exchange student. She commented on how sexy she thought his bright, radiant, green eyes were.

An hour and a half later they were in his dorm room. Stefan thought to himself, amidst the sounds of passionate moaning, drunken kissing, and clothes being removed, that his life was pretty great.

The day was going by just as Bradley feared it would—slow and stressful. Early on in the day, he decided he was definitely going to get drunk after work, but hadn't yet made up his mind if he was going to call in the next day. Clearly, being the shipping manager for a meat processing plant wasn't the career choice he'd envisioned for himself.

Bradley grew up in the typical, American middle-class, suburban family; not exactly rich, but nowhere near the poor house. From an early age, right on through high school, he was always one of the popular kids, as if it was ingrained in his DNA from birth. By his sophomore year, he was the starting halfback on the varsity football team. His junior year, the college scouts were already showing interest. Everything was set up perfectly for his senior year.

Then everything fell apart.

Three weeks before his eighteenth birthday, after the third game of his senior season, Bradley was pounding back drinks at the customary, after-game party. The game was a crushing victory. Several college scouts from the biggest schools in the country were in attendance and Bradley did not fail to impress. He ran for the second highest rushing total in school history that night. He was on fire.

It was nearly two a.m. when Bradley and his girlfriend, Jennifer, left the party. She was much less drunk than he was and took it upon herself to drive them both home.

The exact cause of the car crash was never fully determined, but investigators theorized that Jennifer lost control of the vehicle and veered off the road, where it slammed into a drainage ditch and proceeded to roll several times.

Jennifer was thrown thirty feet from the car and was pronounced dead on arrival. Bradley survived, but had sustained severe back, leg, and knee injuries.

He never played football again.

That very same night, almost at the very exact same time of Bradley's car crash, Stefan Herrera, a seven pound, eight ounce baby boy, was born to parents Federico and Esmerelda.

Stefan woke the next morning with a slight

hangover, last evening's conquest still sleeping peacefully beside him. In the new morning sunlight he discovered her to be a real beauty—even more so than he originally thought the night before.

And he couldn't wait to get her out of his room.

Stefan didn't see himself as a womanizer—he was very straightforward with every woman he was with. He wasn't looking for anything long term, just some quick, unattached fun. If they were good with that, then great. If not, then he wasn't interested.

He got up from the bed, put on a pair of sweatpants, and left to take a shower. He returned fifteen minutes later to find Megan awake and lying on her stomach. She'd tossed the covers aside, exposing her naked flesh to the warm sunlight. Seeing her there on the bed, Stefan knew he couldn't just let her leave.

After a quick round of morning sex, the two of them got dressed and ready for their respective days. Megan proposed breakfast, to which Stefan respectfully declined. Lunch he may have gone for, but he rarely ate breakfast. Before leaving, Megan wrote down the number of the hotel she and some friends were staying at, mentioning that he should give her a call in the next few days.

He briefly considered throwing the number away after she left, but decided to hold on to it. She did mention she had friends.

He thought he just might call her back.

Bradley woke up, not hung-over from the previous night's drinking, but still drunk from it. Needless to say, he called in sick to his job. It wasn't so much that he couldn't have gone in—he'd actually shown up a little tipsy several times before.

This was different. He knew he needed a break and that he'd be calling in Friday as well.

He went back to bed and slept until almost noon. He was quite relieved, and more than a little surprised, to find that he wasn't hung-over. He got up and fixed himself a small meal and ate in the silence of his apartment. After eating, he took a long, hot shower. He caught a glimpse of his face in the bathroom mirror and thought he should shave. Every year there was more gray in his beard and thinning hair. It made him look much older than his true age.

Above his left eye he noticed a scar. *How the hell did I get that?* he wondered. He hadn't noticed, or even thought about the scar in years. He spent the entire time in the shower trying in vain to remember how he got it.

Bradley plopped down on the sofa in his living room, still damp and naked from the shower, and browsed through the adult section of the cable guide. It took him nearly five minutes to find a movie he hadn't seen.

With the rest of his evening planned out, Bradley got comfortable on the sofa and started the movie.

La Terrazza was very crowded, as Stefan stood at the bar and ordered drinks for himself and his new female friend he'd met earlier that night. After a tough day of classes, he was ready to unwind and have some fun. A young woman approached him as he was ordering and introduced herself, speaking as if he already knew who she was. When he replied that he didn't know her, she responded with frustration, bordering on open hostility. She interrogated him

~ 83 ~

about calling her back and accused him of using her for a quick screw. Stefan could tell she was intoxicated and tried to diffuse the situation, calmly explaining to the woman that he didn't know who she was.

Her reaction to his calm explanation was to empty the contents of her drinking glass directly into his face. From the taste, Stefan figured it to be a cosmopolitan of some sort.

In the club's restroom, Stefan wiped the mix of alcohol and fruit juice from his face. He checked his reflection in the large mirrors hanging on the wall in front of the line of sinks and wiped the paper towel through his hair and across his forehead, over the scar above his right eye. He remembered exactly how he'd gotten it; the only blemish on his otherwise perfect face. Soccer practice, twelve years old. He was moving in to block his friend, Jeraldo Salazar, when their heads collided. Stefan received ten stitches, Jeraldo lost a front tooth.

He hadn't thought about that day in years.

When he returned from the restroom the date he'd come to the club with was nowhere to be found. He left not long after and headed home.

Bradley's phone rang. The caller id brought up his work number. It was the second day in a row that he'd called into work and he figured they were calling to inform him that he was no longer employed there. He let it ring a few times, wrestling with the notion of whether he should answer it at all. He finally gave in and answered after the sixth ring, ready to give a piece of his mind to whoever it was on the other end of the line.

But to his surprise, it wasn't someone calling to give him bad news. It was Sarah Davis.

Sarah was a coworker who had a fling with Bradley before she shacked up with her current man. She said she was calling to check on him, since he'd called in the past couple of days. He lied and told her everything was fine, that he was just feeling a bit under the weather. She asked if he would mind if she stopped by after work. He replied that he wouldn't.

Four hours later, Bradley rolled from atop Sarah. She hadn't been at his place for more than ten minutes before they started pulling each other's clothes off. They never made it to the bedroom and ended up having sex on the living room floor. He had no idea why she was there and wasn't about to ask. All he knew for certain was that it was the happiest he'd felt in a long time.

They had sex two more times that night, once more on the floor, and once in Bradley's bed, before falling asleep for the night, wrapped in each other's embrace.

Stefan prowled the hallways of the Ibis Murcia Hotel looking for room 307. After the disastrous flameout of the previous evening, he decided to call Megan. She invited him over to their hotel room for some drinks and fun, and mentioned that if he had any friends that wanted to come, he should bring them along as well.

He decided to come alone.

Megan's two friends were just as attractive as she was. Stefan explained that none of his friends were available to come, which was an outright lie, as he never asked any of them to begin with. The room was filled with booze and there was a fair amount of marijuana being passed around. Stefan learned the girls were leaving the next morning on their sightseeing trip and this was their farewell party to Spain.

Stefan joined right in with the party, having a good sample of the alcohol, weed, and, eventually, the girls too. It was his first time with multiple sex partners and afterwards he could definitely attest to it not being overrated.

Bradley woke up alone in his single bed. He rolled over to find Sarah in the bathroom, fixing her hair and doing her makeup. He asked her where she was going, to which she replied that she was heading back home to her fiancé. When he questioned her about the previous night, her response was that last night was a quick fling, and nothing else. She was upset with her man and she needed a night away. She didn't expect anything else from Bradley, nor did she want anything. Before leaving, she told him she might stop back by from time to time.

Bradley cried in bed for close to an hour after she left. He'd never felt more worthless in his whole life than he did at that moment.

He dried his eyes and came to a decision. He decided today would be the last day anyone would use him, or humiliate him, or treat him as if he wasn't a living, breathing human being. For tomorrow, he was going to kill himself.

The rest of the day was devoted entirely to pleasing himself. He ate his favorite foods, listened to his favorite music, and watched his favorite movies. Anything he enjoyed doing, he did.

He stayed up until almost midnight before falling asleep, bringing to an end what he was certain would be the last day of his life.

The train ride from Murcia to Madrid seemed to take much longer than it normally did. Stefan chalked it up to dreading the coming day. Every Sunday since his father had passed, he made the trip to attend mass and have brunch with his mother. Brunch he didn't mind. Sunday mass, on the other hand, he could do without. Not that he couldn't use it. He had plenty to repent for—that was to say, if he actually repented.

The day was always ended the same—Stefan counting down the minutes until it was time to depart for his train, his mother always trying to get him to stay and visit just a little bit longer. On the rare occasion he would give in to his mother's supplications, but mostly he would come up with some excuse as to why he had to leave. He always felt a little guilty and sad about leaving his mother, but the hour-long train ride back home usually alleviated any bad, lingering feelings.

After mass and brunch, he visited with his mother for close to three hours, his longest visit in the past two months. When it was time for him to leave, Stefan gave his mother a long hug and a big kiss on the cheek. They exchanged I love yous and Stefan told her he'd see her next week.

Had Mrs. Herrera known it would be the last time she would ever see her son alive, she would've thought of something else to say to make him stay longer.

He stared at the makeshift noose hanging from the ceiling fan and worked up the courage to step up onto the chair sitting beneath it. Bradley had no idea how to tie a slipknot and had done the best he could with the little bit of rope he could scrape up from his apartment. There were much more efficient ways of killing himself, but hanging was the only method besides jumping from a tall building, or slicing his wrists, that he had access to. And neither of those options sounded too appealing.

He stepped up onto the chair and put the loop of rope around his neck. Many thoughts raced through his head, as he temporarily considered not going through with it. But the mess that was his life was too much of a burden for him.

A burden which he knew he couldn't carry alone.

With tears streaming down his face, he slipped one foot from the chair seat, soon followed by the other.

His ineptitude at tying a slipknot, however, caused the noose to slide down and strangle him, instead of quickly snapping his neck. His hands flew up to the rope, and Bradley immediately regretted his decision. His legs flailed back and forth as he tried to free himself. He clutched at the rope tightening around his neck, desperately trying to lift himself up to relieve the tension. Ten seconds turned to fifteen, fifteen to twenty, until Bradley started to feel his body go limp. His fingers tingled and his legs twitched at the lack of blood and oxygen. His hands could no longer grasp the rope and his arms fell to his sides. Consciousness was fading and everything was going to black, when the ceiling fan finally gave way to the added weight and frantic thrashing.

Bradley crashed to the floor below, the ruined ceiling fan and busted plaster falling down on top of him. He gagged and coughed, ripping the rope from around his neck, glad to be alive. Several minutes passed as he composed himself, taking in short, ragged gasps of breath at first, followed by longer, drawn out wheezes.

He cried on the floor for a long time, debris still littered all over him, before his attention was taken by the sound of his ringing phone. He hurried to it, desperate to hear another person's voice—any person's voice. His mother greeted him from the other end of the line.

They talked for close to a half-hour, Bradley wisely not mentioning the suicide attempt. His mother could tell there was something wrong by the sound of his voice, but could not get him to open up. She asked if he was still going to make it to the cookout next weekend. He replied that he would, already looking forward to it in his mind.

They said their goodbyes and I love yous and Bradley hung up the phone.

He cleaned up the mess in his living room, the whole time trying to think up a good excuse as to why the ceiling fan collapsed.

Once he finished cleaning, he drove to the corner gas station to pick up a quick dinner and a few other things. As he drove, he decided tomorrow would be the day that he turned his life around. And the first thing he was going to do was quit working his horrible job that he could no longer stand.

Stefan boarded the train to Madrid in a huff, not pleased that he had to go to work on such short notice. The intern for Monday was sick and they absolutely had to have a replacement. Stefan had no choice in the matter. He was technically an employee and he knew the most about the project. He had to go, whether he liked it or not.

He took his seat and buried his nose in his book, just as he did on every trip. Normally, he would have hardly even looked up during the ride, but that day he only made it fifteen minutes in before closing the book and looking around the passenger car.

To his direct right sat an elderly couple. Across from him, two businessmen. To his rear right, a mother and her two children.

And to his front right sat two gentlemen, speaking in a language foreign to Stefan's ears. They were dark complected; Stefan figured them for Spanish or Middle Eastern descent. They looked fidgety and anxious, like children waiting for their parents to leave the room before doing something bad.

The man closest to the isle reached down, cigarette lighter in hand, and very discretely, lit something on the back of his shoe on fire.

Stefan sprang from his seat, shouting what he'd seen as he did, and pulled the man to the floor of the isle. The two businessmen who had been sitting across from Stefan, turned to find him wrestling on the floor with the suspicious man, whose friend was getting up from his own seat, box cutter in hand. They pounced on the other man before he could get to Stefan, who was extinguishing the fuse on the suspicious man's shoe. Several others came in to help and within a matter of seconds both suspicious men were subdued.

A bloody box cutter was pried away from the man Stefan had fought with.

Stefan tried to stand, but promptly fell back to the floor, bleeding profusely from his back, chest, and abdomen. People rushed to his side, using shirts, jackets, scarves—anything they could find to try and stop the bleeding. Some yelled to stop the train, while others ran off to get help.

But there was no help to be had for Stefan. The damage was far too great to overcome. He gasped several times for air, blood streaming from his lips. A man kneeling next to him squeezed his hand and said a prayer. Stefan squeezed back, looking him directly in the eyes. The man assured him everything was going to be alright.

Minutes later, Stefan Herrera died.

Bradley woke up to the sound of his alarm clock, a little sadder than he normally was. He had no idea why, only that he was. It felt as though he'd lost something very precious to him, and he knew he'd never get it back.

He considered shaving again before showering, but like the day before, he decided against it. His facial hair would help cover the welts and rope burn from the previous day.

Following his shower, Bradley sat down on his couch with the first cup of coffee of the morning and watched the news, while simultaneously putting his shoes on. They were just finishing up the weather forecast and preparing to go to commercial. He was only half listening as the newsman and woman teased the upcoming stories. *A residential fire on the Southside kills two. Why running too much could be detrimental to your health. A terrorist plot foiled in*

Spain. What really goes on aboard public school buses and how to keep your children safe.

Bradley finished putting his shoes on, got up from the couch, and headed into his bedroom. He took his keys, wallet, and two crumpled pieces of paper from the nightstand and returned to the couch.

The newscasters returned from the commercial break with the winning lotto numbers.

4. 16. 28. 42. 23.

4. 16. 28. 42. 23.

Bradley checked the crumpled ticket five more times before fully comprehending what had just happened.

He'd just won eighty-million dollars.

He half yelled, half laughed as he jumped up from the couch, the winning ticket clutched firmly in his hand. He started to shake and fell to his knees, crying and laughing with uncontrollable joy.

While Bradley celebrated, the newswoman reported on a breaking story out of Spain, which focused on the heroic actions of a young college student, who was killed while thwarting a terrorist plot to blow up a commuter train.

Had he been watching, Bradley would've seen the young man's face, a face that looked remarkably similar to his own. Others that knew him when he was younger would've said that the young man on the television was a dead ringer for a young Bradley. An almost perfect twin.

But Bradley didn't see his face. In fact, he would never see his face.

He picked up his phone and dialed his mother's number, eager to share in his new, good fortune.

Daggoth the Destroyer

(I love the idea of the supposed inherent-evil of heavy metal music. Fascinated is a better description. Heavy metal and horror just seem to go together, so it's kind of a no-brainer. This is a take on that, as well as the terrors of being a kid in high school, which is a horror story all on its own. I'm also in love with the idea of a shared universe. I drop little things in some of my stories to connect them to other things I've written. This story has two such instances: my two fake bands, Astral Cross and, to a much smaller extent, Wingnut.)

HALLOWEEN MORNING

Andy Copeland sat down on the edge of his bed and started the painstaking process of stripping off all the heavy metal band patches that were scattered across his worn, filthy jean jacket. It was a difficult process, as Andy had always preferred the sew-on patches to the iron-on type. He felt they looked better and were much more durable. Removing them seemed to be the best option to adequately clean all the dried mud and pig feces that caked every square inch of the jacket.

He slid the hobby knife beneath the first patch, the logo of the band Slayer, and carefully started to cut the stitching. He moved slowly, not wanting to accidently slice the patch, or worse, himself. As he cut, his only thoughts were of the ones who had done this to him. He envisioned them getting ready for their annual Halloween bash they had every year. They had no idea what was in store for them.

After he finished with the first patch, Andy immediately started on the next one. At this rate, he figured, it would only take him a couple hours to finish stripping them all from the jacket. It was tedious work, but Andy didn't mind. It made him feel like a warrior, preparing his armor for battle.

As he began removing the next patch, Andy smiled at the thought of the hell he was going to unleash.

THE PREVIOUS DAY

Andy opened his school locker and switched out his textbooks, preparing for his last class of the day—Agriculture. He hated the class, but it was a requirement to graduate and the only other alternative was shop class, which interested him even less than agriculture. The only bright spot of taking the class was that he got to see Cindy one last time before the end of the day. They only shared two

~ 94 ~

classes that year, so the last class was always the highlight of his day.

He had known Cindy Mills since the fourth grade, when her family moved into the house next to his. Over the next three years, they became best friends and often hung out and played together. But before their friendship could blossom into something else, Cindy's family moved away and they inevitably drifted apart.

Once they entered high school, she began to hang out with a new crowd. They were what the stoners called "preps," and their ranks consisted of mostly rich kids and jocks. The two of them remained friends, though not nearly as close as they once were. And once Cindy started dating one of the football players, Andy knew his window had closed. But he never gave up hope that someday Cindy would be his.

"Here you go dude," came a voice from behind him. He turned to see his cousin Ricky, whose outstretched hand contained a cassette tape. "Hot off the presses."

"That's awesome," said Andy, taking the tape. "I can't believe I got a copy of this. I can't wait to listen to this."

"Yeah, it is awesome. I listened to it last night. You won't be disappointed. But listen, don't go making a bunch of copies of it. It doesn't come out for another couple months and if it gets back to my brother that I gave anybody a copy, my ass is grass."

"Don't worry. The only person who's gonna hear this is me. Besides, I think the only people in this school who like this stuff are me and you," Andy assured his cousin. It had been Ricky who first got Andy interested in heavy metal four years earlier, when he played him the new Iron Maiden album, *The Number of the Beast,* and from that moment Andy was hooked. He listened to nothing but metal from then on. And the heavier it was, the better.

Andy turned back to his locker and grabbed a notebook and two cassettes.

"What are those?" asked Ricky.

"Oh, these are... uh... copies of the new Poison and Bon Jovi records that just came out," replied Andy.

"Poison? Bon Jovi?" mocked Ricky. "Don't tell me you listen to that faggy shit. You ain't turnin' queer on me, are you?"

"No," Andy shot back while closing his locker. "I made them for Cindy."

"Whoa, whoa, wait a second. You made her copies of those shitty records? Where'd you get them?"

"Danny made me copies."

"Bullshit. Danny hates that crap. No way he had those. Please tell me you didn't buy those shitty records just to make her copies of 'em?"

Andy's silence let Ricky know he was on the right track.

"Jesus, dude. Can't you see... She's not into... She's just using you?"

"You don't even know her," Andy shot back.

"I know enough to know that she's using you."

"Whatever," said Andy, hoping to switch the subject. "Hey, you coming over tomorrow night?"

"No I can't," replied Ricky. "Parents are taking me with them to some lame-ass Halloween party. I can't get out of it."

"Man, that sucks," said Andy, before taking a look at the clock in the hallway. "I better get goin'. If I'm late to Ag one more time, Mr. Pearson said he was personally gonna call my dad. See ya on Monday."

"See ya," said Ricky, as Andy started to walk away. "Remember: no copies."

Andy gave him a thumbs up sign without turning around, acknowledging his friend's reminder. He made his way as quickly as he could to the Ag building, beating the bell by mere seconds, avoiding Mr. Pearson's wrath. The building itself was no more than a little shack where the class would meet before heading outside to begin the day's assignment. Andy was not overjoyed when Mr. Pearson announced what they would be doing that day: working at the hog pen. Without a doubt it was the one thing he hated most about the class, and with the chance of rain at zero percent, there was no way to get out of it. The only thing that made the crappy news easier to take was the sight of Cindy, sitting two seats across from him.

She'd really blossomed since Andy first met her all those years ago. Gone was the gangly, rail-thin, boyish figure, having been replaced by voluptuous curves. Her teeth, which seemed to have spent a lifetime hidden behind metal, were now perfectly white and straight. And her hair, which had spent its adolescence in an infinite ponytail, was now the gorgeous, silky mane that Andy feasted his eyes upon daily. The girl next door that got away from him was now a beautiful young woman.

Andy daydreamed about her frequently, and as with any other young man going through the growing pains of puberty, they were mostly of the sexual nature. Not all of them though, but even the ones that didn't always inevitably returned to where they began: with the two of them having passionate sex.

Andy was smack-dab in the middle of one of these daydreams when Mr. Pearson signaled it was time to head outside and begin the day's class.

"Mr. Copeland?"

Upon hearing Mr. Pearson utter his name, Andy snapped back to reality to discover he was the only one still seated. This garnered a good chuckle from the rest of the class, especially the jocks.

"Mr. Copeland? Are you going to join us today?"

"Uh... yeah. Sorry," Andy said, quickly gathering his things, before following the rest of the class outside.

The hog pen was located about a hundred yards away from the Ag building. It was an unseasonably hot day for early spring and Andy found himself starting to sweat under his denim jacket. The heat also did nothing to help the smell emanating from the hog pen, and the closer the group got to it, the more overwhelming the smell became.

Once there, Mr. Pearson divided the students up into two smaller groups: one to handle and move the bags of feed, and the other to distribute the feed to the hogs. The first group consisted of the stronger kids in the class, which included Kevin, Cindy's jock boyfriend. Andy was a part of the second group that was made up of the girls and the weaker kids in the class, which didn't bother him because it gave him more time to spend with Cindy.

"Hey Cindy," Andy said, walking over to one of the feed troughs where she was working.

"Oh, hi Andy," she replied, barely stopping her work to acknowledge him.

"So, I... um... I made those tapes you wanted," he said, taking the tapes from his jacket and handing them to Cindy.

"Oh wow, that was fast," she said, taking the tapes. "You didn't waste any time, did you?"

"Well, I didn't have much going on last night, so I went ahead and put 'em together. There was some room left on the tapes, so I put some other stuff you might like. L.A. Guns, a new band called Warrant, Def Leppard—"

"Def Leppard? Oh, I love them. That new song of

theirs... What's it called? 'Hysterical.' It's great."

"Yeah, 'Hysteria.' That is a great song," Andy said, correcting Cindy, who was unaware that he had even corrected her at all. "So, what're you... what're you doing for Halloween?"

"I'm going to a party out at the Farm. The football team's putting it together. What are you up to?"

"Not much. I was supposed to hang out with my cousin, but he canceled on me. I'm probably just going to hang out at the house."

Cindy looked around and noticed a couple of her friends looking her way, whispering and giggling to each other. She turned back toward Andy. "Well, I better get back to work. Thanks again for the tapes."

"No problem. If... you know... need anything else just... uh... you know, give me a call. I'm usually home."

Cindy nodded at Andy, then turned and walked over to her friends. Andy watched her walk away and then headed back to the barn to get more feed.

"Hey Andy?"

Andy looked over his shoulder, toward the sound of Kevin's voice. He and the other jocks were standing near the pickup truck, its bed full of feed sacks.

"Come on over and give us a hand with this stuff," said Kevin.

Andy walked over to the group. "You sure this is okay?" he asked. "Mr. Pearson put me in the other group."

"Oh yeah, he'll be fine with it," assured Kevin. "He went back to the classroom to get something and he left me in charge. And you look pretty strong. We could definitely use the help.

"Besides," Kevin continued, as he gave Andy a couple playful jabs to the stomach, "you don't want to work with the girls and those wimps all day, do you?"

"No, not really," said Andy, smiling.

"Alright then, grab one of these bags here and follow me," said Kevin, grabbing a feed bag from the bed of the truck.

Andy walked to the truck to pick up one of the bags, but despite his best efforts, he could barely move its seventy-five pound bulk. Kevin, who was watching the scene play out, dropped his own bag and walked back to the truck.

"Here, let me help you with that," he said, lifting a bag from the truck bed, dropping it not so gently on Andy's shoulder. Andy winced a little at the impact and initial shock of the weight, but tried his best not to let it show.

"Let's go," Kevin said, lifting his own bag back up onto his shoulder in one quick motion.

Andy struggled to keep up with the rest of the group, the weight of the bag ground into his shoulder and made each step feel as though he had concrete pads on the soles of his shoes. But he was bound and determined not to fail. This was his chance to prove to everyone he wasn't the little wimpy kid they all thought he was.

A couple moments after the rest of the group had entered the barn, Andy lurched inside and dropped the bag of feed to the ground, much to the relief of his throbbing shoulder.

"Wasn't so bad, was it?" asked Kevin.

"No, it was alright," Andy replied, masking his pain.

"So, I got something to ask you Andy," said Kevin. "I saw you over there talking to Cindy a few minutes ago. So what... uh... were you two talking about? I mean, I ain't got anything to worry about, do I?"

The question surprised Andy. "What? No... no,

it's not like that. We're just friends. I was just giving her some tapes I made for her, that's all."

Kevin moved in closer. "Really? You sure there wasn't something else going on?"

"Yeah... I mean, no. No, th-that was it," Andy stammered. "There's nothing else going on?"

Kevin smiled a big smile and backed away from Andy. "Yeah, I guess you're right. I mean, what would she see in a pussy like you anyway?"

The other boys in the barn started to laugh and Andy's heart sank, as he realized he'd been set up. Amidst all the laughter, one of Kevin's buddies spoke up.

"What's that?" he asked Andy. "Hey Kevin, I think this little twerp call you a homo."

"No I didn't! I didn't say anything," cried Andy, his pleas falling on deaf ears.

"Is that right?" Kevin replied. "You know what I think fellas? I think Andrew here is a little too clean cut. Time to put some dirt on him, don't you think?"

A chorus of approvals came from the crowd of jocks. Andy tried to run, but his attempt to escape was futile. The mass of older stronger boys grabbed him, lifted him above their heads, and quickly made their way to the hog pens.

"Put me down, damn it!" Andy cried. "Put me down!"

Andy's shouting attracted the attention of the other group that was working nearby.

"You heard him boys," said Kevin. "Put him down."

The burly boys carrying Andy walked him over to the hog pen and tossed him over the fence. He landed on the ground with a wet thud, sinking a few inches into the soggy, muddy earth.

The jocks laughed and carried on as Andy wiped the filth from his face, in shock by what had just happened. It wasn't the first time he'd been humiliated at school, far from it, but this was easily the worst thing that had ever been done to him. He saw the other group walking up behind the jocks. Several of them were pointing and laughing at him. Andy couldn't see Cindy, but he was sure she saw everything.

Then Andy saw one of the jocks picking the cassette Ricky had given him up from the ground.

"Look at this Kevin," said the jock. "The dork must've dropped it when we threw him over."

Kevin took the tape from his buddy and looked at the label on the case. "Astral Cross? All you dorks listen to the same crap. It's gonna rot your brain."

He pulled the cassette from its case and swiftly snapped it in half, tossing the broken pieces into the mud. Andy looked at the broken, unspooled tape and then up at the crowd around him.

They were all laughing.

He finally caught a glimpse of Cindy. A faint smile grazed her lips, as Andy's eyes settled on her. And what started as a simple smile turned into a full laugh.

"What the hell is going on out here?" came Mr. Pearson's voice, somewhere behind the group. They all turned in unison to see the agitated teacher hurriedly walking toward them. Kevin spoke up before anyone else.

"Andy here was goofing around on the fence, sir, and ended up falling in," he lied. "I told him to knock it off and get back to work, but he wouldn't listen."

"Really?" asked the skeptical teacher. "Then why were you all of you standing around here laughing at him?"

"Well sir, he did fall into a big pile of pig crap," said one of the other jocks. "It was kinda funny."

"Is that right? Let's see how funny you think a

week's worth of detention is, Mr. Rokowski." Mr. Pearson looked around the group. "Anyone else think it's funny?"

He received no takers.

Mr. Pearson climbed over the fence, helped Andy out of the muck, and the two of them headed toward the main building. The rest of Andy's day went by in a haze—taking a shower, getting dressed in an oversized gym uniform, and bagging up his muddy clothes in a black trash bag. He didn't bother telling Mr. Pearson what really happened. He knew nothing would happen to the jocks. The school's football team was undefeated and had a real shot at making it to the state finals. They weren't going to jeopardize that for some poor kid who nobody cared about.

But none of that even mattered to Andy. The only thing he could focus on was seeing Cindy's face, laughing right along with the rest of them. He'd never felt more crushed and humiliated. One of the few people he thought he could trust, a person he cared most for, had betrayed him.

After he had showered and dressed, Andy, toting the trash bag of dirty clothes, walked home. Mr. Pearson had offered him a ride, but he declined, deciding he'd rather walk.

Andy arrived home to an empty house. A note tacked to the refrigerator, along with a twenty dollar bill and the number to the local pizza place, let him know his father would be working late. His mother had passed when he was still a young boy and his father never remarried, or for that matter, even dated anyone else. It was just the two of them, and Andy had long ago gotten used to coming home with no one there to greet him.

He left the kitchen and retreated to his bedroom. Over the years, it had grown to become more of a sanctuary, a safe haven from the cruel world of high school he experienced every day.

Pictures of his favorite bands adorned nearly every inch of the room's walls, and were beginning to stretch their way to the ceiling. Alice Cooper lovingly caressed his pet boa constrictor, Megadeth's mascot, Vic Rattlehead, looked down from a nuked-out wasteland, while Judas Priest looked like they'd just stepped out of an S&M shop. They were the kings of the misfits, consolers of a generation of lonely, forgotten kids—kids that they themselves used to be. It was in these people and their music that Andy found something that he could understand, and in turn, something that could understand him and what he was going through. Something that would never leave him, never abandon him.

They would never betray his trust in them or his companionship.

Surrounded by the pictures of his idols, Andy dropped the garbage bag of soiled clothes on the floor, sat down on his bed, and started to cry.

Astral Cross was one of Andy's favorite bands. They weren't his absolute favorite—that distinction belonged to either Kiss or Iron Maiden—but they were high up on the list. They were a black metal band from Denmark, whose roots traced back to the early '80s, alongside such black metal pioneers as Venom and Celtic Frost. Their first two records were pretty hard to come by; Andy had gotten copies from Ricky, whose brother lived in Europe and would send his younger brother hard to find records. This included the band's yet unreleased third record, a record that Andy was overexcited to finally get to listen to, which now set in a broken pile of plastic and unspooled tape on the desk in his room.

Andy sat down at the desk and began the long process of putting the mangled tape back together. He started with untangling the tape itself, which, despite what it had been through, was relatively unscathed—a few crinkles and bends, but nothing major. After a long, meticulous hour of work, the tape was back where it belonged—on the two small plastic spools.

The tape's plastic casing, however, had been destroyed beyond repair. Out of a stack of cassettes he had sitting on the desk, Andy chose the sacrificial lamb: a barely played copy of an album by the band Wingnut. His aunt had gotten it for him as a Christmas gift and he had only played it a couple of times. They had too much of that "pretty boy" sound for Andy's liking. He took the cassette from its case and began taking the screws from the corners.

Once he had it disassembled, he took the Wingnut tape from the housing and tossed it in the trashcan, replacing it with the newly re-spooled Astral Cross tape. He screwed the two pieces of plastic housing back together, then sat back in his chair and looked at the Frankenstein-esque creation.

Following a moment of silent congratulations, Andy picked the tape up from the desk, put it in the stereo and pressed play.

"Andy?"
"Andy?"
"Wake up Andy."
"It's time."

Andy awoke still sitting at his desk, his head resting on the wood tabletop, a half-eaten pizza and a

~ 105 ~

can of soda resting nearby. He lifted his head and wiped the sleep from his eyes, expecting to see his father. He looked around.

There was no one else in the room.

"*Andy?*"

Andy's head swiveled around looking for the body to go with the voice he just heard. Just as before, he saw no one. The voice was deep, and sinister.

"*Over here Andy.*"

He followed the sound of the voice to his stereo speakers.

"He-hello?" he asked, feeling a little silly that he was addressing his stereo.

"*Hello Andy,*" said the disembodied voice, and the feeling of silliness was replaced by fear.

Andy looked closely at the tape deck. The power was off, yet it was still playing the Astral Cross cassette. Only Andy noticed something was off—the tape was running in reverse.

"I'm dreaming. This has got to be a dream," Andy said to himself. "I'm gonna wake up in a few minutes and everything's gonna be fi-"

"*This is not a dream, Andy,*" assured the voice.

"If it's not a dream, then who the hell are you? What are you doing... talking through my stereo?"

"*Who or what I am is of no concern to you. What I can give to you, however, is.*"

"What you can give to me?"

"*Yes. I know what they've done to you Andy. I know what she did. I know everything. What would you say if I told you I could help you get even with them?*"

Andy paused for a moment. "Why would you do that for me?"

Because I know what you go through every day, Andy. I know you're unhappy. I can make that go away. If you help me, I can help you.

Andy remained silent, offering no answer.

"Think of all the things they've done to you Andy. We can make them pay for all of it. You and me. All you have to do is agree to help me.

"What do you say?"

HALLOWEEN NIGHT

By nightfall the annual Halloween bash at the Farm was in full swing. A large bonfire burned, giving an orange glow to the surroundings, as the high school kids partied, danced, and drank. The sounds of Bon Jovi blasted from the stereo that was set up about ten yards from the fire. The Farm was not so much a farm, more an old cornfield with a bunch of dilapidated barns scattered around it. How it came to be known as the Farm was anyone's guess.

It was near midnight when Andy arrived. His jacket was clean from all the muck and grime that caked it just hours before and the patches were all returned to their original places. He stayed in the shadows and surveyed the area. Almost everyone who'd been in Ag class the day before was there. He spotted Cindy and Kevin standing near the bonfire, laughing and drinking.

To Andy, Cindy was having a great time, hanging out and having fun with her friends. She looked as happy as he'd ever seen her look. She leaned in close to Kevin and kissed him.

Andy made his way around to the stereo, not directly out in the open, but not hidden either. He recognized the Bon Jovi tape in the first cassette deck—it was the one he'd given Cindy the day before. He opened the second tape deck and put his jury-rigged Astral Cross cassette in. He stopped the Bon Jovi tape and started his.

The stereo crackled back to life with the opening strains of the first song.

Daggoth the Destroyer.

The song started ominously, building on a droning organ that was accompanied by a choir of unearthly sounding voices. Andy stood with his back to the crowd of partygoers, who were one by one, beginning to turn toward the sound of the unfamiliar music.

"Who turned off the music?" came a voice from the crowd. "What is this crap?" came another.

Kevin and Cindy turned toward the sound. Even though he had his back toward them, both Kevin and Cindy knew it was Andy.

"Hey wait a sec," said one of the guys standing near Kevin. "That's the kid from Ag class the other day."

The music started to pick up a little; a heavily detuned, distorted guitar came into the mix, playing a slow, bruising riff. Moments later, the song exploded into a full on assault. Andy remained silent, still facing away from the crowd.

"Hey dork?" yelled one of the guys in the group. "It's past your bedtime, isn't it?"

"Yeah, does your mommy know you're out this late?" asked another.

"No she doesn't, 'cause she was at my house earlier sucking my dick for five bucks," came another reply from the crowd, which drew much laughter. But Andy paid no notice. He stood perfectly still, back to the crowd.

"Leave him alone," pleaded Cindy.

"What? You got feelings for the little dweeb?" asked Kevin.

"No... I... he's an old friend of mine," Cindy

replied. "Don't be so mean to him."

"Come on, babe. We're just gonna have a little fun," Kevin said. He turned to a few of his friends. "Let him finish though," he chuckled. "This is too good."

Everyone in attendance gathered around Andy to see what he would do. They were all giggling and snickering as the music died back down to an eerie crawl, reminiscent of something from an old horror movie. A single voice came in over the music, speaking in an unfamiliar dialect. In a call and response manner, Andy repeated everything the voice said, word for word.

Te illumno sa gren-na.
Drak-ni ent zarro ezzenal.

Andy finally turned to face the crowd. A few of them gasped at what they saw. His eyes, from pupil to the whites, were deep red, like blood from a fresh wound. Dark lines ran under his eye sockets, making it look as if he hadn't slept in a few days. His face was gaunt and bony, as if his skin had been stretched over his naked skull. His lips were dry, cracked, and pale, and a white foamy substance poured from his mouth as he spoke.

"All right freak-o, you made your point—you're weird. Now knock this crap off or I'm gonna come over there and kick your ass," yelled one of the jocks. Andy did not respond.

Prini ent suca-ra bocca.

"I don't like this Kevin," whispered Cindy. "There's something wrong with him."

"Yeah, there is," Kevin agreed. He turned to look at one of his buddies. "Mark, go over there and turn that noise off. After that, I want you to kick the shit outta that geek and get him the hell outta here."

Cindy grabbed her boyfriend's arm and jerked him around to face her. "Kevin, goddamn it, listen to me. Something's wrong. I know Andy, he doesn't do things like this."

"I know there's something wrong with him. Your little friend there's a complete fucking spaz and he's ruining the party. Believe it or not, this may help the little dork. Maybe if we kick his ass enough he'll start acting like he's normal."

Hasa boccdini zree-ka te trepedis ot Haval.

Andy did not acknowledge Mark, as the jock walked around him and toward the stereo. The older boy was a little frightened of what was going on around him, but tried not to let it show. The last thing he wanted was for the other guys to know he was scared.

Mark pressed the stop button on the cassette player. It did nothing. He hit the eject button. Still nothing. "Dude, it's not shutting off," he yelled back at Kevin.

Andy and the voice spoke in unison, growing louder and louder with each passage they spoke.

"Just turn it off, damn it," Kevin replied.

L'Chaka oc te zarro.

Pause, fast forward, rewind.

L'Chaka oc te tunda-ra.

All nothing. Thunder boomed from the night sky. Mark backed away from the stereo, fully freaked out by the scene.

L'Chaka oc te destricino.

"Andy, please stop," pleaded Cindy.

Daggoth resi-ra.

"Listen to her geek. Take your freak show and go home," threatened Kevin.

Daggoth resi-ra.

"Hey Kev? This is startin' to freak me out man," said Mark.

Daggoth resi-ra!

The thunder cracked loud, as a lightning bolt

tore through the sky and struck Andy in the top of the head. His body crumpled to the ground in a lifeless heap, his hair smoldering from the impact. A wide array of exclamations poured from the crowd of onlookers, who were undoubtedly shocked by what they had just witnessed.

"Oh my God! Andy!" yelled Cindy, who was about to run to her friend's side, but was grabbed by Kevin.

"Jesus Christ. Somebody... check on him," said Kevin, unsure of what to do. Mark moved in to check on Andy's shattered body. The smell of burning hair and charred flesh made his stomach turn to where he was sure he was going to throw up. He reached down and took hold of the Andy's limp arm, putting his fingers to the wrist.

"Oh shit man. He ain't got no pulse," yelled Mark.

"Are you sure?" Kevin nervously asked.

"Yeah, I'm sure. The fuckin' kid's de-"

Andy's arm twisted beneath Mark's grip and his hand clasped down on the older boy's forearm. Mark screamed and fell to the ground as Andy snapped his forearm like a twig, the bone splintering from beneath the skin.

Andy's metamorphosis was fast and violent. His clothes tore at their seams, as he rose up from the ground, a good two feet taller than his usual five-foot-six. His hands stretched out and reformed, fingers turning into elongated claws. Knees snapped, buckling inward, like the hind legs of an animal and his skin smoldered and cracked as if it were on fire, turning a sickly, grayish-black color. Finally, his face split in two, erasing any trace that Andy had ever existed, revealing a horrifying death mask of gristle, teeth, and menace.

Ferocious red eyes stared; the beast scanned the

crowd, letting out an immense roar.

Pandemonium took over. Kids screamed and ran in every direction, away from the monster. Fire exploded from the ground, negating their escape. The beast surged forward, killing and dismembering everyone in its path. Severed heads, arms, and legs littered the ground in the wake of the beast and some of the kids decided to brave the perils of the fire.

They fared no better.

Kevin dragged Cindy around by the hand, looking for a way through the white-hot flames. Deciding it was too risky to stay out in the open, they headed toward the only shelter held within the confines of the fire: an old, run down barn.

The couple entered the building, the echoes of their friends being murdered behind them in the night. Moonlight peaked through the cracks in the roof, while light from the fire found its way through the rotted planks of the barn's walls. Even with all the light seeping through, the barn was anything but well-lit. Kevin and Cindy found a quiet, dark corner and hid in the shadows, listening to the death unfold outside, until, at last, there was silence, save for the few whimpering voices of a few other kids who had taken shelter in the old barn as well.

The calm was soon broken however, by the sound of hoarse, jagged breathing.

The beast smashed through the barn door, sending splinters and big chunks of wood flying everywhere. Screams broke out through the barn, pinpointing each of the screamers locations. Cindy almost screamed herself, and certainly would have if Kevin had not grabbed her and put his hand across her mouth. The frightened girl shuddered and cried at the sound of the beast doing its grisly business. Kevin held her tightly and whispered in her ear.

"It's going to be alright, okay? It's going to be

alright. We'll wait here until it's gone. It can't see us; it doesn't know we're here, okay? We'll wait all night if we have to," Kevin said, as the last screaming voice was extinguished and all was silent again. They sat in the shadows and listened as the monster made its way out of the barn. Kevin let out a sigh and relaxed his grip on Cindy's mouth, his hand wet with her tears. He turned her gently by the shoulder to face him.

"It's okay. We're just gonna wait here for a while, then I'll check to see if it's clear. Then we'll-"

The beast's arms shot through the wall directly behind Kevin, its massive claws taking hold of the young man. Cindy screamed and fell backwards, helpless and in shock. Kevin shrieked in pain and fought to free himself from the massive claws, which dug deep into his mid-section, gouging and tearing his flesh. The beast jerked backwards, pulling Kevin through the wall. It lifted the young man up from the ground by his arms, bringing him up to match its eye level. The beast moved its demonic face in close to Kevin's and stared the boy down.

"Fuck you... bastard," Kevin struggled to speak, blood trickling from his mouth. In a final act of defiance, he spit square in the monster's face.

The beast reared its head back and let out a fierce roar. It opened its mouth wide and bit down on the top of Kevin's head, digging its sharp teeth into his flesh and cracking his skull. The young man tried to scream, but what came out was more of a wet whimper. The monster pulled back, severing the top of Kevin's head with its powerful jaws. His body went limp as the beast swallowed the crushed skull and brain matter.

Cindy exited the barn, hysterical and unaware of Kevin's fate, or the whereabouts of the monster. All around her on the bloodstained ground the dismembered bodies of her friends lay. The fire that circled the area died down and vanished as quickly as it had begun, leaving everything in silence and darkness.

"Hello? Kevin?" Cindy whispered into the darkness. She received no answer, except for the sound of chirping crickets. She scanned the area for several seconds. There was no sign of Kevin, and, more importantly, no sign of the monster. She spotted the row of cars parked in a nearby field and wasted no time running toward them. Kevin sometimes left his keys in his truck, and as she ran, Cindy was hoping he'd done so this time.

She made it to the truck and looked through the window, the keys dangling from the ignition just as she had hoped. Her hand fell upon the door handle, just as she heard the terrible sound of raspy breathing behind her. She turned slowly to see the hulking beast towering over her. She didn't bother to scream.

"Andy? Andy, please if you're in there, I'm sorry for everything they've done to you," she pleaded. The beast looked at her, but did not attack.

"Andy, I've always been your friend," said Cindy, tears starting to flow. "Please let me go. I-"

The monster grabbed her by the throat and violently slammed her up against the side of the truck.

"No... Andy...," the monster said, in a slow, drawn-out growl. Cindy screamed as the beast opened its massive jaws.

I Think Her Name Was...

(I wrote this little piece for inclusion in a horror-themed anthology dealing with stories based on rock and roll lyrics. Without the song I based it on as a point of reference, this story doesn't make a whole lot of sense. I figured most of the other contributors would chose hard rock or metal songs, which is why I went with the Beach Boys' "Help Me Rhonda" was the song I chose, and I twisted the theme of the lyrics as if they were written by a serial killer. So, go grab the lyrics for that song, read them, then read my story and see how they mesh together.)

SEPTEMBER 14th

She caught my eye the first day I saw her. It was at the park. It was a sunny day. Like the day I met Shelly.

Or was it Sally?

She was jogging. Her hair was pulled up in a ponytail. Constricted. I fucking hate ponytails.

Rita used to wear a ponytail. I used to tell her how much I hated it.

Probably why she isn't around anymore.

They all leave me.

But not her. This one I can tell. She's different than all those other whores. Screwing around on me with other guys.

But not this one. This one can make me forget all the others.

I think her name is Rhonda.

SEPTEMBER 16th

I got in late last night and cried myself to sleep. I need Rita so bad. I mean Rhonda.

I dumped Shelly last night. She didn't take it too well. She cried a lot.

I think I'll meet Rhonda in the park again today. Maybe I'll finally get up the guts to ask her out.

I hope she's not wearing her ponytail. If so, I'll have to keep my mouth shut about it. You know what they say about first impressions.

Gotta wash the clothes today also. Van too.

SEPTEMBER 17th

I talked to Rhonda yesterday. It didn't go so well. She told me she was married. Stupid. I never noticed her wedding ring. I told her about Shelly and how we were supposed to get married, but she ran off with someone else. She told me she was sorry to hear that. I don't know if she was genuine.

I don't know, maybe she was.

She was wearing the ponytail. I had to dig my fingernails into my palm to control myself. I hate ponytails. Makes women look less feminine.

Sally used to wear ponytails. I used to tell her how much I hated it.

SEPTEMBER 18th
Drove by Rita's place—Rhonda's place yesterday. Shit, it's hard keeping track of all the names.

There used to be an Amanda too, if I remember correctly. Yeah, there was. I remember I used to sing that Barry Manilow song to her.

Mandy.

It used to make her cry. Toward the end, that's all I was good for—making her cry.

SEPTEMBER 21st
I've decided to abandon my plan of getting with Rhonda. She is married, after all.

I met a new girl over the weekend anyway. Her name is Cindy. We'll be going out tomorrow night. Hopefully it all goes well. We met at the gym. I'm not a member yet. Just scoping the place out. If we hit it off maybe I'll join. I do need to lose a little weight. I'm getting to be that age where I need to take better care of myself.

I hope Cindy can help me forget about Rhonda.

Or was it Sherry?

Did I mention I dumped Shelly the other night? The same place I dumped Rita and Sally.

They were all there.

SEPTEMBER 23rd
I think my date with Cindy went well. I picked her up at the mall. She had some shopping to do before we went out.

I only had to yell once. She told me she loved me. We didn't have sex though. My mother used to say that girls who gave it up on the first date were whores.

Cindy's definitely not a whore. I think she could be the one.

SEPTEMBER 28th
I'm having serious second thoughts about Cindy. Everything started off good. She told me she loved me, now she won't hardly speak to me. Every day I fight the urge to just fucking dump her.

I can't stop thinking about Rhonda. It was a mistake to think that Cindy could take her place.

I decided not to join that gym. I don't really have time for an exercise regime right now.

SEPTEMBER 30th
I dumped Cindy last night, which technically would've been this morning, since I did it around two a.m. I just couldn't be around her anymore. She cried a lot. Pretty much all the time. She was much different than the person I first met. I just can't deal with that kind of negativity around me right now.

I think I'm going to go back to the park tomorrow.

OCTOBER 2nd
I spent the whole morning in bed thinking about her. I saw her yesterday at the park. She was still wearing the ponytail, but I didn't mind. I hadn't seen her in such a long time.

She's the one I want.

I cleaned out the back of the van today. I found some of Cindy's old things. She may want these. I might drop them off later.

On second thought, she probably doesn't need them anymore.

I had to get a new shovel. Mine busted the other night. The ground's starting to freeze. Winter must be coming sooner this year. Getting harder to dig.

Especially through the first few inches of ground. I might have to come up with another plan.

I picked up some extra zip ties while I was out. Was beginning to run low.

I'm thinking about joining that gym again.

OCTOBER 4th

I didn't see her at the park today. It was raining. It doesn't matter though; I know she's the one I want. I can feel it. It might take some persuading on my part, but I'm sure I can get her to love me.

Tomorrow is the day. She's the one who can help me forget all the others.

I think her name is Rhonda.

Or was it Rita?

Long Time Listener

(Years and years ago, I was pretty much forced to listen—by my stepfather—to the Rush Limbaugh show. He was a big-time Rush fan. That's where the genesis of this story came from.)

"See folks, this is the stuff I'm talking about. This is the byproduct of the liberal, touchy-feely crap that's shoved down our throats by the media, day in and day out," Harry O'Leary barked into the studio microphone. The ultra-conservative shock jock was deep in the middle of his daily call-in show and he was on a roll. That day's topic was one he really had a problem with—behavioral disorders. "A.D.D., A.D.H.D., A.P.D., Aspergers—it's all a bunch of bologna. And then we're compounding the problem by feeding them Ritalin and all this other junk. Well I ain't buying it. All we're doing is turning these kids into mindless, soulless, zombies just to cure hyperactivity, when all they need is a swift kick in the pants. Back in my day, you didn't have all this crap. You had good kids and bad kids. The bad ones got the paddle at school and the belt when they got home. Simple as that. It seems to have worked out fine for my generation. You sure didn't hear about kids taking guns to school and killing their fellow classmates. Something's really screwed up in this country folks, and it's up to us to fix it. I'm a father of two, with one more on the way, and neither of my girls act like some of these kids act now. And neither will my third one, which I'm secretly hoping is a boy. I really hope my wife isn't listening. I think she's wanting another girl.

"So, I want to hear what you all think. Let's head back to the phone lines. Hello caller, you're on the air."

"Hello Mr. O'Leary. Long time listener, first time caller," came the monotone, characterless voice on the other end of the line. "I wanted to discuss today's topic with you for a few minutes, if you wouldn't mind."

"I wouldn't mind at all caller. That's kind of what I get paid to do for a living. Do you have a name sir, or should I just keep calling you 'caller?' "

"You can call me... Chris, if you like."

Harry shook his head, not knowing what to make of the monotone-voiced man and the peculiar way in which he spoke. "Okay... Chris, what do you have on your mind?"

"First, I wanted to *compliment* you on having such a terrible, hate-spewing, radio show. It never ceases to amaze me how certain people hide behind the first amendment to alleviate themselves of any responsibility for the words they spew from their diseased mouths. Second, I'd like to say your assessment of behavioral disorders is... *interesting*, to say the least."

Normally when Harry had the occasional confrontational caller, he'd waste no time giving him the "O'Leary Salute," which was the pre-recorded audio of a male voice telling the offending caller where he could go, and what he could do once he got there. Today however, Harry decided to engage the caller on his own. "Well *sir*, and I use that term *very loosely*, that first amendment which you referred to gives me the right to say whatever the hell I want to say, whenever I damn well please. Thousands upon thousands of service men and women have died to grant me that freedom and I'll be damned if I'm going to let someone like you tell me I'm, in any way, wrong for exercising that privilege.

"Now I wanted to keep this civil, but, by insulting me, you obviously have no desire to do that. You're trying to paint me as the bad guy for having the balls to stand up for what I believe in. If you hate me and my show so much, why are you even bothering to listen? Correct me if I'm wrong, but every radio comes equipped with a volume and station knob. Do me a favor—quit being a dick and turn off my show, you liberal, leftist, commie."

Harry waited several seconds, fully expecting to hear a rebuttal. He got nothing except dead air.

"Hello? Caller? Are you still there, or did you hang up in protest of my radical views?"

"No. I'm still here," Chris said finally, in an even, calm voice. "I am curious though... Shouldn't you be giving me the 'O'Leary Salute' right about now?"

Harry chuckled. "You read my mind sir. You know, I'd say it's been a pleasure, but it really hasn't. So without further adieu—"

"You hang up on me and this bitch dies!"

Chills shot down Harry's spine at Chris' vehement declaration. Through his studio headphones, he could hear the muffled sounds of a woman crying. He also heard what he thought to be a child's voice. They both sounded as if they'd been gagged.

Harry stammered and tried in vain to come up with something to say. Chris beat him to it.

"I'm... sorry for that unfortunate outburst. But I had to make you aware of the severity of your actions. You never know when the resident psycho is going to phone into your radio show."

"Well, let's all just calm down," Harry said, as he motioned to the studio engineer in the control room to call the police. "I... I know you're upset with me and I'll admit some of that is completely my fault. I... apologize for that." The words burned in his throat as he choked them out. Harry didn't like to apologize for anything, even if it meant he might save a few innocent people. "I know you don't really want to hurt anybody, so let's just—"

"You're wrong," Chris cut him off. "I'm not upset with you. In a strange way, I really admire you. The way you can just... say things and not worry about it. The freedom that must come with. And... I *do* want to hurt people. I've learned a lot about pain in my life. I think it's time I shared what I've learned."

"Yes, I understand Chris, but... come on, you must want help right? Why else would you call into my show? You must want help." Harry made his voice sound as earnest and soothing as possible. "Let me help you Chris. Let those people go and let me help you. Together... we can get through this." As he said the words, Harry saw his future expanding before his eyes. If he thought he was famous before, this was going to put him off the charts, and into Oprah territory after this.

Especially if he could talk the psycho out of killing his hostages.

On the other end of the line, Chris was silent for several moments. "Chris? Hello?" Harry said into the microphone. "Are you still there Chris?"

"My father would've loved your show," Chris' voice finally crackled back to life. "I... don't know if he was a republican or not, but... you and him could've probably been brothers. Or at least best friends. He died about ten years ago. In a fire. My mother died on my twentieth birthday. A guy I met one time told me that anyone you know who dies on your birthday, you inherit a part of their soul. I don't really know if I believe him. He was kind of a drug addict. Probably dead now, too. I know I don't believe I've become more like my mother. She was a very tolerant person. She had to be to put up with my father, who was a notorious womanizer. Did I mention she died of cancer? Horrible disease. It always seems to strike at the best of us, while people like myself, and you, and my father, we all get a free pass, able to screw, and lie, and cheat... Cause pain.

"Laugh as much as you breathe; Love as long as you live."

A puzzled look came over Harry's face. He'd heard that phrase somewhere before. He didn't have time to comprehend its origin however. "Chris, let me tell you from experience, it's never that bad. I'm sure that deep down your father loved you and your mother very much." He was lying of course, but he made it sound convincing. "I feel like I've been brought here to help, by some kind of divine intervention, or whatever you want to call it. You called me Chris. You called me. Let me help you."

"You... can't... help... me. It's not as if I'm a busted piece of furniture or a broken toaster that can be taken apart and fixed. This isn't about my childhood, or my upbringing, or my parents. My father never abused me. He was an asshole, no doubt about it, but he didn't put lit cigarettes out on my arms, or lock me in a closet for days on end. That's not what all of this is about. I am simply a man who's been pushed to the brink by the society he lives in. And now, I've found the only way I can make people understand... is to push back."

The gagged woman's voice could be heard in the background. It sounded to Harry like she was trying to scream, and he feared the psycho was definitely doing, or about to do, something to her.

"Bu-but... answer me this Chris," Harry said, trying to pull Chris' attention away from his captives. "Why take hostages? You can make your point without harming innocent people. You don't need to do it like this."

"When you make peace with yourself, you can make peace with the world. Very touching." Like before, Harry was absolutely sure he'd read or heard that somewhere. Chris continued. "You still have no idea, do you? Why do you think I called your show?"

"I think you called my show because you wanted to make your point. Life's been hard to you and even though you don't want to admit it, I think you want help. Maybe not from me, but from someone listening. Someone—"

"I could've called any show in the U.S.A.!" Chris angrily interrupted. "I could've called anyone else— CNN, Howard Stern, the fucking Today show. Why did I choose your show? You know the answer. You know the answer!"

Harry bit his lip in anger. He wanted desperately to tell this asshole to fuck off, but knew that if he did, it would mean the end of his career and possibly the end of human lives. "I... I don't know Chris. I need you to tell me, so we can—"

"Freedom is one of the deepest and noblest aspirations of the human spirit," Chris interrupted.

Laugh as much as you breathe; Love as long as you live.

When you make peace with yourself, you can make peace with the world.

Freedom is one of the deepest and noblest aspirations of the human spirit.

It all became suddenly clear to Harry.

An inspirational picture hanging on a wall. A scrapbook full of family memories. A bust of the fortieth President of the United States, Ronald Regan.

"No... No, no, no, no. This... it can't—"

"Yes. I assure you it can, Harry," Chris interrupted. "I have to show people what happens to true innocents of this world. The people of this world who only try to do good. This place destroys them. Like cancer. Which one shall I destroy first?"

"No! No, no, no! Don't please! Please just talk to me," Harry pleaded.

"If you won't choose, I'll have to choose for you," Chris said, the sound of the crying woman and her children rising in the background.

"LEAVE MY FUCKING FAMILY ALONE!" Harry screamed into the mic.

"I'm sorry. That's not a valid answer."

Harry heard the cocking of the pistol. The first shot cracked unexpectedly and he jumped in his seat.

Two more shots followed in quick succession. The phone went dead silent.

Harry screamed incoherently into the microphone.

"And now... you know," came Chris' cold voice through the headphones.

"YOU KILLED THEM! YOU KILLED THEM! I'LL FUCKING KILL YOU! I'LL HUNT YOU DOWN

AND I'LL FUCKING KILL YOU, YOU SON OF A BITCH!"

"Not if I beat you to the punch," Chris butted in. "This is Lucas Christopher Kelly, signing off."

Lucas Christopher Kelly.

The sight of the man's face tore through Harry's brain. His old personal assistant of five years. The same personal assistant he'd fired in favor of a young, pretty blonde woman. The same blonde woman he'd spent countless nights with, while his wife was pregnant with their third child.

Harry was about to say something when the sound of the fourth, and final, shot roared through his headphones, followed by the clack of a phone hitting the ground.

Jimmy's Story (A Deranged Parable)

(I've had the idea for this scene banging around for a while now. I ended up using it in a novel I wrote as well. It's really messed up in a darkly-funny, insane way. I love dark humor and, for the most part, the darker it is, the more I like it. This is based on an actual event.)

Jimmy Palimino put the handgun under his chin and pulled the trigger.

PART ONE: HOW THE HELL DID IT COME TO THIS? (OR, WHAT WOULD DRIVE A RICH, SPOILED BRAT TO SHOOT HIMSELF IN THE FACE?)

Once upon a time there lived a young man named Jimmy. Jimmy grew up in the exclusive town of Brooke Harbor, Massachusetts, the only son of Mr. Anthony and Mrs. Susan Palimino. Like any other only child with rich, enabling parents, Jimmy was a selfish, self-obsessed, spoiled brat.

His father was a workaholic womanizer, who bought Jimmy's love with lavish, expensive gifts. He was a lawyer by trade, but was looking to become more active in the political arena. And like most men with political ambitions, he screwed everything of the opposite sex that walked on two legs and had a pulse. (Everything except the woman he entered into holy matrimony with, that is.) Susan knew he was cheating on her; her preferred method of drowning her sorrows over her husband's infidelities was consuming large amounts of alcohol. It wasn't her only vice; she enjoyed the company of males other than her husband as well. (What's good for the goose is good for the gander). She liked her extracurricular lovers to be on the young side, which worked out nicely once Jimmy entered high school. All his friends used to want to have sleepovers at the Palimino house on the weekends, not so much because they wanted to hang out with Jimmy, but because they wanted to have sex with his mother.

Jimmy's high school through college years were one big, sleazy odyssey, filled with roofies, booze, drug binges, and the occasional orgy. Any trouble that he got into was quickly quelled by his father and his growing political connections. Jimmy graduated from college (also with considerable help from his father) with a degree in business and took a job his dad had set up for him in New York City.

As a graduation present, Anthony got his son a practical, yet highly ceremonial gift that would help in the home security department on the tough streets of New York.

PART TWO: A BRIEF HISTORY OF RUSSIAN ROULETTE (OR, SOMEBODY MUST'VE MISPLACED THE DECK OF CARDS).

The "activity" or "game" of Russian roulette was conceived sometime during the eighteen hundreds. Russian soldiers would force their prisoners to play it and would place bets on who the eventual winner would be. And if they had no prisoners at their disposal, some of the more unbalanced soldiers would actually play it themselves, just to relieve the boredom of being stuck inside during the harsh Russian winter.

The rules of the game were simple: get a revolver, put a single bullet into one of the chambers, spin the cylinder, snap it into place, put the gun to your head, cock the hammer and pull the trigger. If all goes well, your brain matter should still be intact at the end.

Each participant repeats the cycle until one of their luck runs out, in which case a new bullet is put into the gun and play resumes. The whole process is repeated until only one player remains, at which point said player is declared the winner and is allowed to change their pants.

Typically, there are six chambers in a revolver, which gives the shooter a little over a sixteen-and-a-half percent chance of blowing his head off. There are variations of the game that use a gun that has only five chambers, which ups the percentage to twenty. Even more variations exist, like adding a bullet each time through the cycle, to using several different guns that have various amounts of ammo in each.

But of all the variations and changes to the basic rules, there is one common thread that ties every form of the game together: they all use some form of revolver.

PART THREE: THE FATEFUL NIGHT (OR, HOW TO REPAINT YOUR LIVING ROOM ON A TIGHT BUDGET).

Jimmy Palimino sat on his two-thousand dollar leather sofa in the living room of his penthouse, which overlooked Manhattan's Central Park, and entertained his party guests. There were seven people there including Jimmy: four women and three men. The penthouse wasn't the absolute best that money could buy, but it wasn't far from it either. And as was the case with almost everything else Jimmy owned, it was paid for by his father. The group had been out partying earlier that evening and Jimmy had talked everyone into coming back to his place to continue the fun, which was to include getting completely inebriated on booze and drugs, groping the women after they'd passed out, and finally, having an all out drunken gang-bang.

But all of those plans changed when Jimmy pulled out his dad's graduation gift for all to see. A nickel plated, ten shot, .45 caliber semi-automatic handgun, accessorized with a porcelain handgrip, featuring a fourteen karat gold dragon inlay.

"You all are a bunch of fucking pussies, you know that?" Jimmy asked, in his barely coherent, drunken, drug induced slur. "You know how they used to separate the men from the boys back in the old days?"

"What's that bro?" replied one of Jimmy's male friends, after snorting a big line of cocaine off of the coffee table.

"Russian roulette baby. Put the gun to your head and pull the trigger." Jimmy put the gun to his temple and feigned shooting himself. "BAM!" he shouted, causing one of the girls to jump.

"Isn't that dangerous?" asked the least wasted of the female party guests. "And I think you're supposed to use a .38 or something, aren't you?"

Jimmy laughed. "Dangerous? Dangerous? You think I'm afraid? What the fuck do you even know about danger, bitch?" Jimmy shouted, as he grew more agitated. "I ain't afraid of anything! I ain't afraid of this gun, I ain't afraid of you, I ain't afraid of my father, I ain't afraid of nothin'! So fuck you! Fuck all of you! You wanna see how badass I am?" Jimmy put the gun under his chin. "You wanna see? I'm gonna show you! I'm gonna show you all what I'm made of!"

Jimmy pulled the trigger. The top of his head popped open like a jack-in-the-box toy, and his friends got a real good look at what he was made of. Blood and brain matter splattered everything in close proximity. The walls and ceiling looked like a ghastly version of a Jackson Pollock painting. Jimmy's body slumped sideways on the couch, as his friends understandably freaked out. Jimmy was, in fact, quite dead. (He did put a loaded gun to his head and pull the trigger. What exactly did you think was going to happen?)

So, where did he go wrong? First, being loaded on alcohol, coke, weed, and ecstasy probably wasn't a good start. Second, and most important, Russian roulette is dangerous enough when it's played with a revolver. When it's played with a semi-automatic pistol, it tends to be called something else: suicide. Barring a misfire, Jimmy had approximately a 99.7% of shooting himself.

THE MORAL OF THE STORY: If you happen to be a rich, spoiled brat, with a misplaced sense of entitlement, and you like to get high and play Russian roulette in your drug induced trances, please, use a revolver. It's much safer.

Spies Like Us: The Wild and Crazy Rock 'n Roll Tale of Wingnut's Ride Through Sex, Drugs, and Assassinations

(From the pages of
Metal Sledge Magazine)

(This is straight-up, Chuck Barris stuff here. I was fascinated by his story and I found myself wondering one day, "A rock band would be a perfect cover for something like that." Another story written as a fake magazine article. I actually created a fake name for myself while writing this: Johnny Slaughter!)

Los Angeles-2009

"When you're deep undercover, infiltrating a military base, knowing if you get caught you'll be tortured and killed, well, compared to that writing a four minute rock song doesn't seem that hard," says J.J. Lange, as we drive around town in his '65

Mustang convertible. It is a warm June day and Lange is ready to reminisce.

"I remember our first time playing L.A. It was a fucking crazy gig. We played the Roxy. It was our first show in the states. We all decided to play the encore in the nude. Completely bare-ass naked. It was nuts.

"We'd been touring for a couple years already, but we'd never played in the states. All our shows were overseas, for obvious reasons, you know. But with metal becoming so popular around that time, the Agency felt we needed to become even more of a 'functioning' rock-and-roll band than we already were. And that meant playing shows everywhere, even places where we didn't have any missions going on. When we started, we only played cities where we had something going on. We never played just to play. But with all the publicity the bands of that era were getting, we had to live the part almost twenty-four seven. Our real lives became the disguise after a while, you know?"

The agency Lange is referring to is the Central Intelligence Agency, and the band, which Lange was a founding member of, is Wingnut. In the 1980s, Wingnut, along with every other metal band, rode the wave of sex, drugs, and rock-and-roll. But unlike other bands, when the after-show party ended for the members of Wingnut, it didn't include passing out with a dozen groupies in a haze of sex and booze.

Well sometimes it included that, but most nights were spent inside stuffy vans gathering intel or going through paperwork and surveillance video.

"I remember plenty of nights I spent in the back of a smoldering-hot surveillance van, jerking off into a paper towel, while Rikki and Jami were back at the hotel doing God-knows-what to the groupies we brought back with us from the show," J.J. pauses.

"And some of those European chicks… they'll do just about anything."

    Two weeks ago, the surviving members of Wingnut reunited (minus founding member Lance Banzi and second lead singer Johnny Throttle) and gave a tell-all interview to the network news show *NightLine*. In the interview, they confirmed long standing rumors that they were, in fact, C.I.A. operatives. (The C.I.A. quickly denied their claims. They also declined to have any involvement with this article.) The rumors got their start in the early '90s after founding member Jami Blazen quit the band. (Several people I spoke to, including members of the band believe it was Jami who spread the rumors. Jami has flat denied this.) During the *NightLine* interview the band came clean about their entire history.
    "I believe it started somewhere around '75," said bassist and founding member Ougie McDaniels. "Quicksilver was the codename for our operation. They originally intended to start it up back then, but the touring industry at that time was still in its infancy. People were still trying to figure out how to do it efficiently. It wasn't until the '80s came around that everything started to come together."
    According to the members, the band was "formed" in late '81 by the C.I.A. to perform covert missions in other countries. These missions included intel gathering, infiltration, surveillance, and assassination. The guise of rock band was chosen partly because of the travel (most bands toured half of the year, all over the world.) and partly because the Agency thought no one would ever believe a bunch of

idiot rock-and-rollers were government spooks.

"It was a great plan," said singer Jami Blazen. "They were right. *Who would believe* we were world class spies and assassins?" The answer: nobody.

During the late '70s, early '80s, heavy metal looked like it was on the way out. Punk and New Wave had taken over the rock-and-roll world, while Disco dominated the charts. Ozzy Osborne had quit Black Sabbath, Led Zeppelin broke up after the death of John Bonham, and both Bon Scott and Keith Moon died early deaths. It seemed as if every band that had a hand in creating the genre was either breaking up or losing their relevance.

And some think this is exactly the reason why the C.I.A. chose the genre in the first place.

"[The C.I.A.] never wanted us to get big," recalled Jami. "The idea was to keep everything really small. The lower the profile, the easier it would be to keep everything under wraps."

But something happened in the month of November, 1983 that changed all of that: Quiet Riot's third album, *Metal Health*, went to number one on the Billboard charts.

"That was the game changer," said J.J. "After that record it seemed like every band in the metal genre was getting a lot more attention, including us. I remember releasing *Hellbound Express* (the bands second record) in July and it sold like 5,000 copies or something. After the Quiet Riot record went number one, we sold the other 20,000 copies we had printed in one month. That's how fast it all changed. One week, we're just another rock-and-roll band from Noweresville, U.S.A., and the next week their doing stories on us in *Rolling Stone*."

The band went from playing small, dingy clubs to 5,000 seat theaters. To say they weren't prepared for the change was a gross understatement. "We pretty much had to change everything we did," recalled Ougie. "Before, things were much more relaxed, easier going, you know? After everything changed though, we were really under the microscope. It seemed like we had people around us everywhere we went. Everything we did... Somebody was watching."

"To keep the ruse going, we had to start living that rock-and-roll lifestyle almost 24/7," said J.J. "I mean, it used to be we'd get done playing a show and that was it. We'd meet a couple'a fans, sign a few autographs, and then we'd go about our business. Then almost overnight, it was like—BAM! Everything changed. Now we had real dressing rooms and hanger-ons. And groupies," J.J. laughed. "Yeah, that's when we knew things had really changed. When we got pretty girls who wanted to fuck us 'cause we played guitar. That's every guy's fantasy, I think."

According to press releases and interviews, Wingnut hailed from Pocatello, Idaho. In reality, the members of Wingnut hailed from all over the country, and each had vastly different backgrounds.

J.J. Lange was born James Johnston on September 29th, 1959 in Akron, Ohio. "I lead a much different childhood than most rock-and-rollers did. I had one of those typical suburban, all-American childhoods. Nice house, white picket fences, a mom that stayed home and baked cookies. I played sports in school. I was a popular kid."

J.J. played in several garage bands growing up in Akron. "I remember going to see Zeppelin around 1975 and just being completely blown away. I mean just floored. A few of my friends from the neighborhood went to the show too and the day after we all got together and decided to start a band. We didn't get very far though. I think all we pretty much did was sit around and argue about who was going to play guitar because we all wanted to be Jimmy Page," J.J. laughs.

Although he always enjoyed playing rock-and-roll, J.J. kept his feet planted squarely on the ground. "As cool as I thought it would've been to be a rock-and-roll star, I also knew that it was a one-in-a-million chance. And I've never been much of a gambler."

After high school, he enrolled at Ohio State University and pursued a degree in electrical engineering. "I originally wanted to work for N.A.S.A. That was my goal. Computers, in that day and age, were a relatively new science and N.A.S.A. seemed to me to be on the leading edge of that technology.

"That was before a recruiter from the C.I.A. came to visit the campus. And the rest, as they say, is history."

Ougie McDaniels was born Paul Wooten on July 12th, 1958 in Springfield, Illinois. He was a straight A student, carried a 4.0 g.p.a., and was valedictorian of his class. And he was a band geek.

"Yes, I was in band," recalls Ougie. "Pep band, marching band, drum line, jazz band. I did it all." From early childhood through high school, Ougie learned to play the piano, bass, guitar, drums, clarinet, saxophone, trumpet, and the trombone.

"I never did play in any rock bands in school though," Ougie laughs. "I guess I just wasn't cool enough."

Ougie attended college at Harvard and graduated with a degree in criminal psychology. "I applied for work with the F.B.I. and C.I.A. I really wanted to work for the F.B.I., but I just couldn't hack it physically, and ultimately I went to work for the C.I.A."

Jami Blazen, the blonde haired, banshee voiced singer, who looked more like he came from California, as opposed to Idaho, actually did come from California. He was born William Larson on June 17th, 1958 in San Diego. Jami was the first to admit he wasn't a great student. "I was terrible. Well, maybe not terrible. Some subjects I was good at. History, English... stuff like that. Everything else I was either just plain mediocre or straight up bad."

Jami enlisted in the Army after graduating and quickly joined the ranks of the famous Army Rangers. "It was, without a doubt, the hardest thing I've ever had to do. [Training to become a Ranger] was literally a two month descent into Hell. I fractured my hand, got heatstroke a couple of times... and I lost something like thirty pounds."

He joined the C.I.A. after hearing about one of his colleagues joining up. "Yeah, I won't give you his name, but he wasn't that bright of a guy, even compared to me," Jamie laughs. "And to be honest, he wasn't that good of a soldier either. So I thought, 'If they'll hire him, they'll defiantly hire me.' "

The two other members that filled out the band's original lineup were Lance Banzi and Rikki Storm. Lance, whose real name is Carl Banali, was a smart, shy kid, who grew up in Cedar Falls, Iowa. "He was the best musician in the group, hands down. Past or present," says J.J.

"He was not only a classically trained guitarist, but a classically trained pianist as well. And he couldn't stand heavy metal music," Ougie recalls, with a laugh. "I remember when we all first got together, me and him went and bought a bunch of metal records and spent a whole night listening to them. Most of it was pretty idiotic crap, but some of it we really liked. Van Halen, Priest, Iron Maiden. Lance really got into the 'shredders', you know guys like Malmsteen, Steve Vai, Randy Rhodes. He thought those guys were heads above everybody else, especially Rhodes. He wore those first two Ozzy records out."

After a show in Venice, Italy on May 23rd, 1984, Ougie and Lance departed to do a job in Turkey. "Me and Lance did a lot jobs. We worked really well together," says Ougie. "On that job in Turkey, it was a pretty simple—basic intel... surveillance. We spent two days in Bafra scoping the targets, who were housed up in a big warehouse facility. We had everything down—when the guards were there, when they weren't, the positions of their surveillance cameras—the works. On our third night there, which was actually supposed to be our last, Lance was supposed to infiltrate the perimeter and hack into their cameras so we could keep an eye on them from back home.

"He was tapping the last camera when out of the blue one of the guards snuck out the back for a smoke. Lance was standing right there, not more than five feet from the guy. In just a matter of a few seconds there were probably a dozen soldiers outside surrounding Lance. I was positive they were just gonna shoot him right there, but instead they just beat him up a bit and took him inside.

"And me, I was helpless. I couldn't do anything. I only had the basic combat training; I wasn't a soldier. Had Rikki or Jami been there..." Ougie pauses and shakes his head. "I had to leave my friend there. That was the hardest thing I've ever had to do.

"A week-and-a-half later, Lance contacted the agency from a pay phone in Istanbul. I've got no idea what he went through during that time, but I can guarantee you it wasn't good."

Lance never contacted anyone in the band again. He quit the C.I.A. immediately after returning to the states, and his current whereabouts are unknown, though it is rumored that he moved to Montana and went completely off the grid. A press release given by the band at the time said he quit due to inter-band turmoil.

Things didn't fare much better for Lance's replacement, Vinnie Ward, a.k.a. Nathan Vincent. "Vinnie was always more interested in the rock-and-roll lifestyle than the actual part of it all," J.J. recollects. "That's not to say he wasn't good at his job, but it was difficult sometimes to get him to focus."

It was during a mission near the Israel/Lebanon border, that things turned disastrous for Vinnie. "Our job was to basically check up on this new, Islamic terrorist group that had set up shop near the Lebanon border," J.J. remembers. "From the get go it seemed like the whole operation was fucking jinxed. Vinnie's headset wasn't working, my night-vision goggles crapped out. During our parachute drop in my main chute didn't deploy and I had to use the reserve. It was just one thing after another."

Upon reaching their destination, things went from bad to worse. "Long story short, we got ambushed by a patrol in that area. Our intel was bad, so we were thrown right into the frying pan and didn't even know it until it was too late. We were pretty much fucked and the only thing we could do was run.

"I couldn't see anything, I just ran as fast as I could. I heard cars coming up behind me, but I never looked back. I didn't know where Vinnie was—if he was following me, if he got caught—at that point I was just trying to save my own skin."

J.J. narrowly escaped his pursuers, but Vinnie was not so lucky. "After a couple hours of walking, I made it to the extraction point. Nobody had heard from Vinnie. About a week later, it was confirmed that Vinnie was..." J.J. stops, unable to continue. A video in surfaced, depicting the brutal beheading of Vinnie at the hands of his captors.

"We all saw the tape," says J.J. "Rikki and Jami were ready to go in by themselves and wipe those fuckers out. They were really pissed. At first, the Agency didn't act like they were going to do anything about it, but we kinda forced their hand, so to speak.

"A week after the tape came out, Rikki and Jami headed up a strike team and they went into the complex and wiped 'em out. They killed everybody." J.J. doesn't go into details, but rumor has it that Rikki and Jami took some of the terrorists alive (including two who helped behead Vinnie) and proceeded to behead them all, one by one, so that each of them could see what fate was about to befall the other. Supposedly, they videotaped the slaughter and circulated the tape around the Middle East. Jami has no comment on the event.

Rikki Storm, whose real name was Richard Pratchet, grew up in the blue collar town of Harrisburg, Pennsylvania. "Rikki was a *real* blue collar guy," recalls J.J. "I remember when we started to get big and we had roadies and techs to set all of our gear up, he would still go out, incognito, and set his kit up. The rest of us, we were ecstatic 'cause we didn't have to set up our shit anymore, but Rikki was just one of those guys... He just wanted to do it himself. He really took great pride in what he did."

Rikki looked the blue collar part as well, standing 6'2" and weighing around two-hundred and twenty pounds. "He was definitely the bodyguard of the band," laughs Ougie. "He was just a really stout guy. He would tell us all these stories about being in the Marines and it would always end with him and Jami arguing about who was tougher, Rangers or Marines. And this isn't taking anything away from Jami, but when Rikki was around you didn't need any security. I seen him work firsthand. He was all show, and all go."

Over the years, Rikki developed the reputation of a hard partier. "He could party with the best of them," remembers J.J. "He reminded me of that character on 'Sesame Street'. Or maybe it was the 'Muppets'. The one that played the drums. 'Animal' I think was his name. That was pretty much Rikki when he was partying."

In the early morning hours on November 17th, 1987, Rikki's hard partying ways lead to tragic results. "I was the only other member present at the time," says Jami. "We were in Berlin, and our record (1987's *Full Metal Fury*) had just went to number three on the charts. Well, needless to say, me and Rikki had been going pretty hard that night. J.J. and Stevie (Van Saturn, who joined the band in 1986) were out on a recon assignment and Ougie called it an early night, so it was just me, Rikki, some of the road crew, and some groupies, you know, back at the hotel, drinking, partying.

"A bunch of us were in Rikki's room and he grabbed the TV set to throw it out the window. And I'd seen him do this about a hundred times. I thought nothing of it. He threw it out the window and turned around and I could see the cord stuck in his belt. It was like everything was in slow motion. He jerked backwards, hit the bottom of the window sill and toppled out the window. Fifteen-story drop." Jami pauses. "Died instantly."

"I think that was the closest we ever really got to

being shut down," J.J. recalls. "There were a few other times where we thought we might get axed, but when Rikki died, we had our plane tickets back home and our bags packed. We all really thought that was it."

Jami Blazen gives a much different story. "They weren't going to shut us down. They may have threatened it a few times, but that's all it was—threats. And the reason why is really simple—the success rate of the jobs we did and the money we were bringing in. [The C.I.A.] were making a lot of money on us, between the records and touring. And we were doing all the work. For the first few years, we all pulled down our base salaries for the year and that was it. We didn't see any extra. Finally, I believe around '86, we'd had enough and we all threatened to quit if something didn't change." Although details of the deal remain secret, rumors are the Agency cut deals, in the upper seven-figure range, with the band members. "Well, you know I can't comment on that, but... Nobody was unhappy at the end of the day," laughs J.J.

J.J. Lange pulls his car into the parking lot of an authentic looking Mexican restaurant called *Rancho de la Brisas*. "Best Mexican food this side of the border." From the look of the building, I don't dispute his claim. Inside, J.J. and I join Ougie McDaniels and Stevie Van Saturn (a.k.a. Dan Stevens, who replaced the deceased Vinnie Ward in 1986), who were already seated at a table. "Stevie's a really nice, sociable guy," says Ougie. "Until he gets on a job. Then he's one-hundred percent all business. You can't even talk to him. It's weird. He doesn't get mad or anything, he just doesn't talk. But once the mission's over, he's back to normal. He's like a machine."

"He just turns it on and off, like a light switch," adds J.J.

"It's the SEAL training," explains Stevie, who enlisted in the Navy out of high school and became a member of the SEALs. "That's what they train you to do. When you're on a mission, that's the most important thing. That takes total focus."

A couple minutes after J.J. and I sit down, drummer Tommy 'T-Bone' Gilliad (a.k.a. Robert Ackerman) walks in and joins our table. Compared to the other members, Tommy's a big man. Upon first seeing him, I figure him to be a former member of some elite, military unit, like Stevie and Jami. "No, I'm not. I can't fight for shit," laughs Tommy.

"It's true, he can't," Stevie confirms.

"I graduated from New Mexico State with a bachelor's degree in government," says Tommy. "I joined the Agency right out of college. My specialties were profiling and code breaking. Not exactly the next James Bond."

The five of us sit around chatting for about ten minutes when J.J.'s cell phone rings. It's singer Jami Blazen. As usual, J.J. says, Jami's running late.

"Yeah, he has this condition," Stevie deadpans, "it's called L.S.D.: 'Lead Singers Disease.'"

As we wait for Jami to arrive, the other four members start to share stories and talk about being a fully functional rock-and-roll band.

"As strange as this is going to sound, that was the hardest part of the job," says Ougie. "The missions were a synch. We were highly trained professionals at that kind of stuff, so it was second nature. Recording albums, writing songs, playing shows... that was the hard part."

"We really had to work at it," adds J.J. "To keep our cover good, we had to not only *look* the part, we had to *be* the part. When we first got together we rehearsed and wrote songs for almost an entire year. And as we became bigger, we had to even work harder at it."

Behind the covert operations and assassinations, Wingnut was a solid rock-and-roll band. From the high-voltage guitar riffing from their 1982 debut, *Metal Disciples*, to the fury of 1985's *Lightning Fist*, the band blazed a trail of rock-and-roll destruction all through the '80s and into the early '90s.

"We worked hard and we played even harder," Ougie says. The band's hard partying ways and off-stage antics have become the stuff of rock-and-roll legend, but it wasn't always that way. "Starting out, we didn't know what the hell we were doing. We didn't know how rock-and-roll bands acted on the road. It wasn't until we started opening up for other more established bands that we kinda got to see what being on the road was all about.

"And when we were first starting out nobody wanted to get in trouble, so we were really walking the straight and narrow. But you know how things go—one thing leads to another, and then that leads to another, and so on and so forth. But really, as long as we pulled our missions off, the Agency pretty much left us alone to do what we wanted."

Except drugs. "We had a very strict 'no drug' policy," says Stevie. "Alcohol was fine. We could have as much booze as we wanted, but drugs were strictly forbidden. We had regular random piss tests. The kind you couldn't fake."

"To be as authentic as we could, we had fake drugs backstage," laughs J.J. "We'd cut up powdered milk or powdered sugar and we'd snort it like cocaine. It's the same stuff they use in movies and it looks totally legit. We had fake joints, pills. Nothing too heavy, but it totally sold us. The hardest part was keeping all the people hanging around backstage from trying the stuff."

"Yeah, we had to hire people just to watch over our fake drugs," Stevie chuckles.

But the 'no drug' policy didn't stop the band from having fun and partying like the rock stars that they ultimately were. "We got into all kinds of trouble," says Ougie. "Every rock-and-roll cliché you can think of, we did it. And there were a few things we did that nobody had ever done." Ougie recalls a story about a fishing trip Jami went on. "We were playing somewhere in Mexico and we had a couple days off in between shows, so Jami and a couple guys from the crew rented a fishing boat and Jami ended up catching a three foot shark. He somehow got it back to the hotel and, for laughs, decided to let it go in the hotel's swimming pool. Well, you can imagine how that went, it being a fresh-water creature. Half-hour later, the fucking thing sank right to the bottom, dead. And of course there's a big crowd standing around watching all this go on," Ougie shakes his head. "We got into all kinds of trouble for that."

"We were like kids in a candy store," says Stevie. "And really, who wouldn't be if they were in our shoes. That type of freedom is very overwhelming and we all succumbed to it."

The conversation turned to groupies and sex on the road, just as Jami Blazen walks in and sits down at the table. He had just recently celebrated his 50th birthday, and was still sporting that southern California look. He is, ironically, the only member who has longhair in real life.

"This guy, I don't think, never met a groupie he didn't like. Or fuck," laughs Ougie.

Jami whole-heartedly agrees with the statement.

"Oh, yeah. I've done some crazy shit with groupies in my time. I'm not going to go into details, because I'm happily married now and I'd like it to stay that way."

"No, no, no," interrupts J. J. "You're not getting off that easy. This guy used to have this big photo book of Polaroids of girls he slept with on the road. I think it may have been two books. How many was it?"

"No comment," the singer says, a big smile on his face.

The group disbanded in 1998 following the departure of second singer Johnny Throttle, a.k.a. Carl Stump. Throttle, who supposedly is still employed by the C.I.A., declined to be interviewed for this article. The other members all quit the C.I.A. upon the bands breakup.

"We just need to stop," says J.J. "We were burnt out. You think about it, we were doing two jobs at once and we were more or less told that one could not survive without the other."

"Yeah, the writing was on the wall, I guess you could say," adds Ougie. "On the music side, the band was nose-diving. I remember hearing Soundgarden's *Badmotorfinger* for the first time. It was at an after show party, right after it came out. It just sounded so fresh. At that moment I knew we were screwed."

It seemed like overnight we went from playing arenas, back to playing clubs," says Jami. "Grunge just took over everything. And the missions were becoming pretty scarce as well, with the end of the Cold War and the election of Bill Clinton. Everything just changed."

With the resurgence of '80s metal over the past

couple of years though, there's been renewed interest in Wingnut and the other big rock acts of the 80's. The reunion, however, has been anything but smooth. "The Agency has blocked us from doing anything as Wingnut," says Jami. "Technically, they own the name and everything that goes along with it. That's the main reason we decided to go public with our story. Trying to force their hand." I ask all the members if any of them had any input involving the Wingnut greatest hits album titled *All Killer, No Filler,* which is to be released next month. They all reply they didn't. "We didn't get to pick the tracks, didn't get to oversee the re-mastering. Nothing," says J.J. "And we probably won't see any royalties from it either." Presently, they are working to come to an agreement with the Agency and are hoping to write a tell-all book detailing the bands history. "We'll eventually get it done. I'm sure of that," Jami says. "There's too much money to be made on both sides. And we all know that's really what everything comes down to."

There are some in the industry that suspect this is just a ploy to help an aging 'hair metal' dinosaur band reclaim some of its former glory. "Let them think what they want," says J.J. "They won't find anything out there that disproves our story. It is what it is, and it's all true."

While researching for this article, I in fact did look for things to prove or disprove their story. And while I found nothing to prove it, there was nothing I could find disprove it either. The complete lack of any information regarding their claims, good or bad, leads me to believe, at least, that they may be telling the truth.

But today the band is not looking back to the past. They are busy rehearsing to go back on tour as Wingnut, or if need be, under a new moniker. "To be honest, we're not even sure if we want to use that name anymore," Jami says. "There's a lot of baggage that goes along with it. Right now, I'd say we're about 50/50 on it." And even touring's not a complete given, not overseas anyway. "Think about it, we're a band of ex-spooks and we've basically come out and said we've been doing covert ops in other countries for years disguised as this rock-and-roll band. Would you let us back in?

"We've still got the states though." Jami looks away from me as if he's deep thought, then adds, "I don't think we ever did any jobs in Australia. Maybe they'll let us play there too. And Japan." He lets out a big, hearty laugh at this suggestion. "Yeah, Japan. I'm sure we're all still *big* in Japan."

Behold, a Pale Horse

(This is a snippet of a much, much longer piece that I hope to turn into a novel someday. It's full-on, post-WWII noir. This, I think was my first foray into the world of "flash fiction," which is much harder to write than what you'd think. Flash fiction is basically just the process of cutting out all of the shit from your story. Mostly adjectives and adverbs.)

Duct tape. The stuff could be used for almost anything. It's water proof and almost impossible to break. It was designed to tape up ammo boxes during World War II.

The war, John Cole thought, as he looked down at the workbench. He'd learned a lot during the war. How to survive. To block out pain. How to cope with death.

How to kill.

That's what he was best at. Over the years, he came to excel at it and, eventually, acquired a taste for it.

A taste for death.

Behind him, in the dimly-lit warehouse, sat his latest victim. The man had quit struggling a long time ago, realizing he'd never be able to break free from all the duct tape Cole had used to secure him to the chair. The only thing he could do now was beg for his life.

"Why are you doing this?" asked the man. Cole hated that question. A few years back he would've tried to justify his actions to them. That was when he felt what he was doing mattered. But that was back then.

Cole turned to face the man. "Please mister, whatever it is you think I did—"

"I don't care what you did," interrupted Cole.

"Come on man, let's just talk. You don't need to do this."

Cole moved in close to the man. "You wanna talk? Okay. A few years ago a couple guys like yourself picked up a thirteen year old girl right out of her little suburban neighborhood; she was walking home from school. Snatched her right off the street. Broad daylight. After they had their fun, they cut her up and dumped her in a garbage bin.

"When I finally found them, they were begging, kind of like you are now, completely denying what they'd done. At that exact moment, I realized I could never defeat that kind of evil. That no matter how many guys like you I put into the ground, I was never going make any difference. After you're gone, three more just like you will pop up for me to take care of.

"Ever read Nietzsche?"

"Wh-Who?"

"Friedrich Nietzsche. He wrote, 'Beware that when fighting monsters, you yourself do not become a monster, for when you gaze long into the abyss, the abyss gazes also into you.' He was right. I've gazed into the abyss for far too long. Now I can't look away. I've become the same evil I was fighting."

Cole turned and walked back to the workbench. "I told you I didn't care what you did. That's the honest truth. I don't care—because I don't know. I was paid to kill you. You're simply a paycheck to me. I can't change you or make you understand that what you've done is wrong.

"I am an agent of death, and I'm only here to give you what you deserve."

Cole looked down at the bench and found what he was looking for. He turned to face the man, unrolling the duct tape as he walked towards him.

"Duct tape has about a million different uses," Cole said to the man, who had started yelling at the top of his lungs. Cole paid him no attention and continued talking about the grey tape. "I heard this one guy used it to tape his busted windshield back in his car."

Cole stood directly in front of the man, the stretched tape at the ready.

"But you know the one thing I've found it works best for?" Cole asked over the man's screams. He didn't expect an answer, nor did he get one.

As Cole put the tape up to the screaming man's face, he gave him the answer.

"Restraint."

29 Down

(This is one of my "Twilight Zone" inspired stories. I also like to do crosswords. Thankfully, this has never happened to me.)

Lester Grant lived a typical boring life, on a typical everyday street, in a typical suburban neighborhood in sunny San Diego. And today was just another typical Sunday morning, and Lester started it the same way he had all of the other typical Sunday mornings since his wife of thirty-seven years had passed: sitting down at his kitchen table with a nice breakfast and the Sunday paper.

Lester adopted this routine, as well as many others, almost four years ago, based on advice from a friend who had lost his wife as well. The friend's philosophy was simple: find a way to fill up your time, or you'll simply sit around and wait to die as well. And being a retiree, Lester had plenty of time to fill. Of course, he had a couple things working in his favor. One, he was a career military man, which meant he knew a thing or two about habitual living, and two, unlike most men in their sixties, he had the body of a man twenty years his junior.

He leisurely flipped through the paper, as he sat at the kitchen table and picked through his over-easy eggs and wheat toast. He hardly ever bothered to read the whole thing; it was usually just the sports section, the local news, and sometimes, if the mood hit him, the comics. And he always finished his morning ritual off the same way he always did—by grabbing a pencil and doing the crossword puzzles.

There were always two crossword puzzles in the paper, one that was written by the newspaper, and the standard New York Times one. The one written by the paper was usually the easier of the two, and Lester could almost always finish it without much problem. The New York Times one was a different story.

Lester's crossword strategy was like most peoples': scan through the clues and pick out the easiest ones first, which is exactly what he did this day, as he opened the paper to the crossword section and began the easier of the two puzzles.

29 down. "Moby Dick" author _____ Melville.

Lester scribbled the name Herman into the six blank squares and continued to scan.

14 across. Leaving synonym.

At first glance Lester believed it to be the word exiting, but the answer was only five letters long.

Going, he thought, and quickly jotted it down.

34 across. Root beer brand.

Building off the e in Herman, Lester concluded it could only be Stewart's. He'd never actually had a Stewart's root beer before, but he'd heard somewhere that they were one of the best.

42 across. Opposite of me.

Too easy. You.

24 down. Harper Lee classic, _____ a Mockingbird. (Two words)

To Kill.

Lester scanned the puzzle for a few more moments. His eyes moved from the clues, back to the empty squares, and back again. He repeated the process several times.

Something was odd. Off. He couldn't quite put it all together. He looked at the words he had filled out in the squares once again, going over each one in his head, trying to figure out what was so peculiar about the situation.

Going. You.

Stewart's. To Kill.

Herman.

He rearranged the words a few more times, until it became clear to him what was so odd.

Herman Stewart's going to kill you.

Lester stared at the answers in disbelief. He looked back over the clues to make sure they were right, even though he already knew they were. It has to be a coincidence, he thought. It couldn't be anything else. Just a freaky coincidence.

He continued to scan the clues. 18 across. Holmes residence, 221 B _____ _____. (Two words)

Baker Street.

39 down. The Ides of March.

Fifteenth.

After penciling in the last answer, Lester looked at the calendar hanging on his refrigerator.

The date was March 13th.

Lester was sure his imagination was just getting the better of him now. He wasn't the type of person to believe in fortune tellers or prophets. He didn't believe in hidden Bible codes, or Nostradamus, or that anyone had any knowledge of what was going to happen in the future.

But none of that stopped him from getting up from the kitchen table, walking into his living room, and grabbing the telephone book. Curiosity had gotten the best of him. He had to know, to be able to put the crazy idea to rest.

He hurriedly flipped through the pages to the S section, scanning through the names. Simmons, Slaton, Spiker...

Stewart.

He scanned the first names. No Herman.

A wave of utter silliness swept over him. He chuckled to himself at the thought of his absurdity.

But as quickly as it had come, the feeling vanished when Lester saw a name he'd missed at first glance.

Stewart, Thomas H. 1421 S. Baker St.

Thomas H.

Herman. Baker St.

Lester tore the page from the phone book, grabbed his car keys, and exited the house.

Baker Street was located a mere seven blocks from Lester's house. Despite its close proximity, Lester was sure he'd never been down the street before. Nothing looked familiar to him, as he sat in his car, scoping out house number 1421, waiting to catch his first glimpse of one Thomas H. Stewart.

He hadn't given any thought as to what he was going to say or do once he saw the mystery man. Would he walk up and introduce himself? If so, what would he say to the man he'd never met before? Hello, you don't know me, but I'm the town crazy who lives a few streets over and my weekly crossword puzzle told me that you were going to kill me in two days. Oh, by the way, your middle name wouldn't happen to be Herman, would it?

After an anxious hour-long wait, Lester watched a car pull into the driveway. The driver was an African-American man, who looked to be in his mid- to late forties. A sticker advertising the U.S. Navy adorned his rear bumper.

Another one of those fucking Navy queers. Probably a Gulf War vet to boot, Lester thought. Like most of his Marine brethren, Lester looked down on his military contemporaries. They felt the Navy and Air Force's sole purpose in the military was simply to carry the Marines to the sight of the next battle. And the Army, well the Army was only there to clean up the mess. None of them were on the same level as the mighty Marines. And the vast majority of them didn't consider the first Gulf War to be any kind of war at all.

But regardless of how he felt about the supposed Mr. Stewart and his military affiliation, Lester knew he'd found a way in. He exited his car and started toward the house.

"How long did you serve?"

The man looked up from gathering the groceries from the trunk of his car to see Lester walking along the sidewalk in front of his house. "I'm sorry?" he replied, unsure of what the older man was asking.

"The Navy sticker on your bumper. I saw it when you pulled in," explained Lester.

"Oh, right. Seven years."

Lester extended his hand. "Colonel Lester Alan Mallory, United States Marine Corps. Forty years. Retired," he introduced himself, thinking it would be a good strategy if he didn't use his real full name. As a ploy, he used his middle name in his introduction, to try and coax the other man into giving his.

"Thomas Stewart. Petty Officer Third Class," the man said, shaking Lester's offered hand.

Shit, Lester thought, he didn't take the bait.

"Did you see any action while you were in?" Lester asked.

"Gulf War. You?" Thomas replied.

Gulf War, I fucking knew it. "Vietnam. Four tours. '68 to '72."

"Wow, that's some record. Did you just move into the neighborhood? I haven't seen you around here before."

"No, I live a couple streets over. My doc says I need to get more exercise. Decided to give walking a try. My age... you gotta take things a bit slower. You live here long?"

"No, not really. 'Bout a year."

Lester realized his plan of questioning and small talk was getting him nowhere. He would have to take a more direct approach to get the information he wanted. "Well, I'd better let you get back to your groceries. It was nice meeting you. Maybe I'll see you around sometime."

"Same here," Thomas said, as he watched the older man walk away. He returned to the trunk of his car, grabbed the remaining grocery bags, and headed into his home. He closed the front door, glancing through one of its three, small, rectangular windows as he did, and watched Lester walk back to his car, get in, and drive away.

Later that evening, Lester returned to the Stewart house. The night was moonless and dark.

~ 160 ~

Lester's wardrobe matched his colorless surroundings—dark shoes, pants, shirt, and baseball cap. Perfect attire for his after-hours recon mission. He parked his car a block away and trekked through the small patch of woods behind Thomas' house, stopping at the tree line to watch the goings on through the windows.

Thomas was busy preparing dinner. Lester watched him through the whole process of cooking and eating his meal. He obviously lived alone. Single, widowed, or divorced. Lester's bet was divorced.

Lester crouched in the darkness, trying to formulate the next part of his plan when he saw the kitchen light go out. A short moment later, Thomas emerged from the house, got into his car, and drove away. Lester didn't waste any time springing into action.

He was on the back door in seconds flat, checking for any home-security stickers in the house windows. He didn't notice any, but that didn't really mean anything. There was only one real way to find out for sure. From the back of his pants, Lester pulled the .45 caliber pistol he had carried along with him, and, using the butt of the gun, busted out one of the small, rectangular windows that was set into the door. Glass crashed to the floor on the other side.

No alarms. Lester reached his gloved hand inside, unlocked the door, and let himself into Thomas' home.

Lester moved through the small kitchen and into the living room. It was a nice place from what he could tell; clean and well kept, although sparsely decorated. There was little more than a couch, a couple end tables, and a television set in the living room. On one of the end tables, Lester noticed a couple pictures of a young boy who resembled Thomas.

Must be his son, Lester thought. No pictures of a wife.

Divorced, for sure.

He scanned the room for anything that might give away Thomas' elusive middle name, but after a few minutes he'd found nothing substantial and decided to move on. He made his way down the home's only hallway and stopped at the first open doorway. It was a medium-sized room that had been set up into a home office. A shoddy, department store desk sat along the far wall, papers strewn all across it. Lester figured it would be a good place to look and headed into the room. Before he made it to the desk however, something on the wall to his left caught his eye.

A college diploma.

Lester moved quickly to the document in order to get a good look at it, ready to put an end to the mystery of Thomas' middle name.

He read the name, printed on the document in bold, gothic lettering.

Thomas H. Stewart.

Who the fuck was this guy, Harry Truman?

Lester looked around the desk, fumbling blindly through the papers. Most of them didn't have any names on them; others were addressed Thomas Stewart, or simply Mr. Stewart.

A sealed envelope caught his eye.

It was addressed to Mr. Thomas Stewart, but the way it was addressed wasn't what caught Lester's attention. It was the seal and logo of the Central Intelligence Agency in the upper right hand corner of the envelope that did.

Jesus Christ. He's a fucking spook.

The gleam of headlights on the wall startled Lester. He sprang to the window just in time to see Thomas pulling his car into the driveway.

Lester scrambled through the house, bumping and thrashing his way out the back, getting there seconds before Thomas' key hit the front door lock.

The following afternoon was hot. Lester sat in his car, binoculars up to his face, and kept watch on Thomas' home. He'd cracked the windows to relieve some of the heat, but wasn't about to start the car and possibly blow his cover. Besides, the Vietnamese jungles taught him all he needed to know about dealing with the heat. It didn't break him then, it wasn't going to break him now.

From inside the house, unbeknownst to Lester, Thomas was busy watching him. He had seen the car parked down the street around 11 am. It was now close to 1 pm. He had no idea how long it had been there, but knew immediately that it was the same car from the previous day. The windows were tinted, but he knew it was the old man.

Thomas dialed a number into his cell phone. It rang once before being picked up. "Could I speak to Detective Ron Elliot please?" He paused several seconds as the woman on the other end of the line patched him through. "Hello, Detective Elliot... This is Thomas Stewart. We met last night. My house was... Right, 1421 South Baker Street... The reason I'm calling is, I think I may know who broke in."

The knock on Lester's front door caught him by suprise, as he sat at his kitchen table, eating his dinner. He pushed his chair back from the table, stood, and headed toward the sound. It had been almost five hours since he'd left Thomas' home and he had full intentions on going back there after he'd eaten.

Those plans quickly, and unexpectedly, changed, when he saw Thomas and another man standing on his front porch. He opened the front door.

"Hello," Lester greeted them. "Something I can do for you?"

"Hello, sir," the other man spoke up. "Are you Lester Grant?"

"Yes sir, I am. Who's asking?"

"Sir, I'm Detective Ron Elliot. Have you ever seen this man?" he asked, gesturing toward Thomas.

Lester looked at Thomas for a few seconds, feigning deep thought. "Yeah. I believe I bumped into him on the street the other day. I was out walking."

"So you are aware of where Mr. Stewart lives?"

"Yeah, if that was his house."

"Where were you last night sir?"

"I was here. All night."

"Do you have anyone who can vouch for that?"

"No, I don't. I live alone. My wife passed away a few years ago." He fixed his cold stare on Thomas. "What is this all about?"

"Sir, is that your car?" Detective Elliot asked, pointing to Lester's car parked in the driveway.

"Yeah, it is. And without a search warrant, this is as close as you're going to get to it."

"There's no reason to get hostile, sir. We just need to clear a few things up. Now, were you parked around Mr. Stewart's house earlier today?"

"Yeah, I was. There's a nice patch of forest around that area and I like to do a little bird watching there from time to time."

"Bird watching?" Thomas piped up. He was about to continue, before the detective shot him a look.

"I see you've finally grown a pair and decided to speak," Lester addressed Thomas. "Yes. I was bird watching. Is that a crime now?"

"Sir, there's no reason to get agitated. I'm just here to ask you some questions," the detective said.

"Well, I'm done answering your questions. I'd like you both to leave right now."

"Are you sure this is the route you want to go sir?"

"Am I sure this is the route I want to go? Let me tell you something—I've been up to my knees in blood and shit and guts before you two were even a thought. I've seen things so horrible you can't even imagine. So the thought of you trying to scare me with your tough talk is laughable, at best. Now unless you got a search warrant tucked into that pretty little suit of yours, get the fuck off my property." As an exclamation point, Lester slammed the door in the two men's faces. Without looking back, he walked to the kitchen and sat back down to his meal.

This was unexpected. Lester cursed himself under his breath. He'd underestimated Thomas; he let himself get too careless. Now, as a result, Thomas knew where he lived. His home had been compromised and Lester knew he couldn't take the chance of staying there until things were resolved.

That won't happen again, Lester thought. The time for half measures are over.

He glanced at the crossword puzzle still sitting on the table. He pulled it closer and gave it a quick look.

23 across. Optimistic number from the Broadway musical "Annie".

Tomorrow.

Tomorrow it is then.

⊕ ⊕ ⊕

March 15th. The Ides.

Waking up in his motel room that morning seemed like a distant memory to Lester, who hid in the woods behind Thomas' house, as he had two nights prior, and waited for the opportune time to strike. He'd been there since dark and it was now close to 10 pm. Thomas had to go to bed at some point.

But the living room lights still burned. All Lester could do was wait.

Once he put together what Thomas was trying to do the night before, Lester decided it would probably wasn't a good idea to stay at his house, and he checked into the motel. He thought it was very clever the way he used the cop; painting him as the bad guy stalker.

He could kill me anywhere he wanted to now and claim self-defense after that performance, Lester thought.

What he still couldn't put together, however, was why?

It had to be something I did, or saw, during the war. It has to be. But what?

I saw some crazy things over there, but nothing so bad that they'd send some spook after me. Something's not—

Lester had no more time to think. The light from the living room windows went out. From another window, a light flicked on and stayed that way for several moments.

Bathroom.

The house blinked into darkness again and stayed that way for some time. Lester knew it was now or never.

He checked the perimeter thoroughly, making sure it was free of cops, and then slowly crept up to the house, under the cover of darkness. The window he'd busted out on the back door the night before was replaced by a sheet of plywood. So much for the quiet approach, he thought.

It didn't matter now though. The time for subtlety was over. For all Lester knew, Thomas was busy preparing himself for a late night raid on his place.

He readied the .45 and kicked the door in, nearly knocking it clean off the hinges. He moved quickly inside, gun pointed. Through the kitchen, followed by the living room, Lester found nothing. He turned toward the hallway. No movement. There were two doors at the end of it. The one on the right was open. He moved quickly to it.

The bedroom was empty. The sheets and bedspread were thrown off. There was no sign of Thomas.

Lester leveled his gun at the closet door, which was open just a touch. He moved slowly, as to not give away his position, and took hold of the doorknob. He flung the door open and moved in front of the dark opening, ready to fire.

There was no one there.

Oh no. Under the bed.

Before Lester could turn, Thomas was on him. He wrapped his arms around Lester and tried to knock the gun from his grip. The old man countered this by rushing backwards and out through the bedroom door, slamming Thomas back-first into the hallway wall. Thomas refused, however, to relinquish his grip and the two men scuffled down the hallway and into the kitchen.

Lester managed to turn himself around, but failed in freeing his arms. He slammed Thomas into the kitchen bar counter, so hard that it separated from the wall and tilted almost sideways, sending knick-knacks, a small television, and a full knife holder crashing to the floor. The violent action achieved the desired effect and Lester brought the gun up. He never got the chance to fire though, as Thomas, upon seeing the gun, head butted Lester square in the face. The older man dropped the pistol, which skidded off the busted bar top and landed on the floor on the other side of the room.

Seeing the gun hit the floor, Thomas was quick to get around to it. Lester was just as quick however. The two men fought on the floor, each one with a hand on the gun.

They fought and struggled.

Until...

A single shot cracked though the house. Lester rose from the floor. Thomas did not.

"Who the hell are you?" Lester demanded, pointing the gun down at Thomas, who was bleeding heavily from the wound to his abdomen. "Answer me goddamn it!" Lester yelled, cocking the hammer of the gun. "Answer me, or so help me God I'll kill you right now."

"No! No, please," Thomas gasped. "Please... don't. Please."

"Who are you?" Lester asked again, feeling his chest start to seize in pain.

"I'm nobody... Thomas Stewart. I'm an... accountant."

"Bullshit! I saw the papers on your desk. I know you work for the C.I.A. Why are you trying to kill me?" Lester was breathing heavily and started to break into a cold sweat. Hold it together. It'll pass. It'll pass.

"I... I swear to God. I don't know what you're talking about. I'm not... trying to kill you. I do account... accounting work for the C.I.A. I... I don't... work for them. I'm not trying to kill you." Thomas' body tensed up in agonizing pain. "P-please..."

The pistol shook in Lester's hand. "What's your middle name?"

"Wh-what?"

"What's your fucking middle name?" Lester screamed, thrusting the pistol down, in close to Thomas' head.

"It's Henry. It's... it's... Henry."

Henry. Henry? No, it can't be. It can't. It ca-

A fierce pain, unlike any he'd ever felt before, tore through Lester's chest in a burning, suffocating spasm. He stumbled forward, then back, struggling to stay upright.

Thomas seized this opportunity and reached to his right and grabbed one of the kitchen knives that had scattered across the floor during their fight. He tried to lean forward, in an effort to stab his attacker, but the pain was too much. He could barely breathe and from the taste of blood in his mouth, he knew at least one of his lungs had been punctured.

Above him, Lester was losing his fight as well. He wheezed heavily and dropped the gun, both hands clutching his chest.

Seconds later, Lester fell too, straight on top of Thomas, who had the presence of mind to stick the blade of the knife up as Lester fell. If the heart attack hadn't killed the older man, the knife blade piercing through his rib cage surely would have.

The pain of the heavier man falling on top of him was excruciating and Thomas thought he was going to pass out. He struggled, but finally freed himself from the dead man's weight. He pulled himself across the linoleum floor, in the direction of the living room, his arms and hands becoming numb from the blood loss. His destination was the phone sitting on the nearest end table. He could only hope he'd have enough energy left in his broken body to dial.

He got near enough to the table and reached up for the phone, finally snagging it on his third try. He flopped down on his back and dialed 911. The operator picked up after the first ring.

"911, what is your emergency?"

"... I've been... shot..." Thomas spoke into the phone, his voice weak and shaky. The operator asked another question, but Thomas could no longer comprehend.

"... help me... Shot..."

Thomas Henry Stewart closed his eyes.

A small crowd had gathered around the police barricade that surrounded the home of Lester Grant. It was early morning and Detective Ron Elliot made his way to the front door, where his partner, Detective Bradley Giffords, waited for him.

"Find anything?" Ron asked.

"No, nothing. Old guy was a fucking hermit," Bradley answered, as the two of them walked inside the house. "Neighbors said he kept to himself. Didn't go out much. We've been through every room in the house. Bedroom, bathroom, living room—all of 'em—spotless. Only thing we found in the kitchen was a few dirty dishes and an old newspaper on the table."

"You check it?" Ron asked, following his partner around the various rooms of the house.

"Yeah, we flipped through it. Nothing on the old guy and nothing on the vic."

Ron shook his head. "Doesn't make any sense. Why would the old guy kill him? What's the motive?"

"Well, the guy was an accountant. Maybe he screwed the old guy's tax return up. That would piss me off pretty good."

Ron didn't respond. He knew his older partner's sense of humor.

"You know what? We got the 'who' and the 'how.' This guy killed that guy. There's no mystery here. Who gives a fuck about the why?" Bradley said. "And let's not forget, the dude was a Vietnam vet. That's motive enough itself. How many times you heard about one of them crazy fuckers snapping?"

"Yeah. More than once."

"Damn right," Bradley said. "Hey, I got an idea. I saw a little breakfast place up the road. What'dya say we let the crime scene guys finish up here and go grab ourselves some coffee? Maybe a sausage biscuit or something? My treat?"

Ron thought for a moment, and then nodded. "Lead the way."